The Year of the Hare

Arto Paasilinna

THE YEAR OF THE HARE

Translated from the Finnish by
Herbert Lomas

PETER OWEN London
UNESCO Publishing Paris

PETER OWEN PUBLISHERS
73 *Kenway Road London* SW5 0RE
Peter Owen books are distributed in the USA *by
Dufour Editions Inc. Chester Springs* PA 19425–0007

Translated from the Finnish Jäniksen vuosi
First published in Great Britain 1995
English translation © *Herbert Lomas* 1995

UNESCO Collection of Representative Works

ISBN 0–7206–0949–6
ISBN UNESCO 92–3–103031–0

*A catalogue record for this book is available from
the British Library*

*Printed and made in Great Britain by Biddles of Guildford
and King's Lynn*

Contents

Translator's Note

I have made an exception in this translation of using English rather than
Finnish currency. The slight loss of flavour seems negligible compared
with the disadvantage of not knowing the cost of the interesting money
transactions, and footnotes would interfere with the reader's pace and
pleasure. Money values have been updated to the equivalents in 1994.
British weights and measurements have also been used, except in certain
appropriate instances.

1 The Hare

Two harassed men were driving down a lane. The setting sun was paining their eyes through the dusty windscreen. It was midsummer, but the landscape on this sandy by-road was slipping past their weary eyes unnoticed; the beauty of the Finnish evening was lost on them both.

They were a journalist and a photographer, out on an assignment: two dissatisfied, cynical men, getting on for middle age. The hopes of their youth had not been realized, far from it. They were husbands, deceiving and deceived; stomach ulcers were on the way for both of them; and many other worries filled their days.

They'd just been wrangling. Should they drive back to Helsinki or spend the night in Heinola? Now they weren't speaking.

They drove through the lovely summer evening hunched, self-absorbed as two mindless crustaceans, not even noticing how wretched their cantankerousness was. It was a stubborn, wearying drag of a journey.

On the crest of a hillock, an immature hare was trying its leaps in the middle of the road. Tipsy with summer, it perched on its hind legs, framed by the red sun.

The photographer, who was driving, saw the little creature, but his dull brain reacted too slowly: a dusty city shoe slammed hard on the brake, too late. The shocked animal leaped up in front of the car, there was a muffled thump as it hit the corner of the windscreen, and it hurtled off into the forest.

'God! That was a hare,' the journalist said.

'Bloody animal – good thing it didn't bust the windscreen.' The photographer pulled up and backed to the spot. The journalist got out and ran into the forest.

'Well, can you see anything?' the photographer called, listlessly. He had wound down the window, but the engine was still running.

'What?' shouted the journalist.

The photographer lit a cigarette and drew on it, with eyes closed. He revived when the cigarette burned his fingers.

'Come on out! I can't hang about here for ever because of some stupid hare!'

The journalist went distractedly through the thinly treed forest, came to a small allotment, hopped a ditch and looked hard at a patch of dark-green grass. He could see the leveret there in the grass.

Its left hind leg was broken. The cracked shin hung pitifully, too painful for the animal to run, though it saw a human being approaching.

The journalist picked the leveret up and held it in his arms. It was terrified. He snapped off a piece of twig and splinted its hind leg with strips torn from his handkerchief. The hare nestled its head between its little forepaws, ears trembling with the thumping of its heartbeat.

Back on the road there was an irritable revving, two tetchy blasts on the horn, and a shout: 'Come on out! We'll never make Helsinki if you hang around in this wilderness! Out of there, sharp, or you'll find your own way back!'

There was no reply. The journalist was nursing the little animal in his arms. Apparently, it was hurt only in the leg. It was gradually calming down.

The photographer got out. He looked furiously into the forest but could see nothing of his companion. He swore, lit a cigarette and stamped back on to the road. Still no sound from the forest: he stubbed his cigarette out on the road and yelled: 'Stay there, then! Goodbye, nutcase!'

He listened for another moment but, getting no reply, stormed into the car, revved up, put the clutch in and shot off. Gravel spat under the wheels. In a moment the car was out of sight.

The journalist sat on the edge of the ditch, holding the hare in his lap: he resembled an old woman with her knitting on her knees and lost in thought. The sound of the motor-car engine faded away. The sun set.

The journalist put the hare down on the grass patch. For a moment he was afraid the leveret would try to escape; but it huddled in the grass, and when he picked it up again, it showed no sign of fear at all.

'So here we are,' he said to the hare. 'Left.'

That was the situation: he was sitting alone in the forest, in his jacket, on a summer evening. He'd been well and truly abandoned.

What does one usually do in such a situation? Perhaps he should have responded to the photographer's shouts, he thought. Now maybe he ought to find his way back to the road, wait for the next car, hitch a lift, and think about getting to Heinola, or Helsinki, under his own steam.

The idea was very unalluring.

The journalist looked in his wallet. There were a few banknotes, his press-card, his health-insurance card, a photograph of his wife, a few coins, a couple of condoms, a bunch of keys, an old May Day celebration badge. And also some pens, a notepad, a ring. The management had printed on the pad *Kaarlo Vatanen, journalist*. His health-insurance card indicated that Kaarlo Vatanen was born in 1942.

Vatanen got to his feet, gazed at the sunset's last redness through the forest trees, nodded to the hare. He looked towards the road but made no move that way. He picked the hare up off the grass, put it tenderly in the side-pocket of his jacket, and left the allotment for the darkening forest.

The photographer drove to Heinola, raging. There he filled up the tank and decided to book into the hotel the journalist had suggested.

He took a double room, threw off his dusty clothes and had a shower. Refreshed, he went down to the hotel restaurant. Vatanen would certainly appear there soon, he considered. Then they could talk the whole thing through, sort it out. He consumed several bottles of beer and, after a meal, moved on to stronger drinks.

But there was still no sign of the journalist.

Late into the night he was still sitting in the hotel bar. He contemplated the black surface of the bar counter in a mood of angry regret. As the evening had gone by he had been mulling over what had happened. It had dawned on him that abandoning his companion in the forest, in an almost deserted neighbourhood, had been an error. Supposing the journalist had broken his leg in the forest? Might he have got lost? Or stuck in a bog? Otherwise, surely, he'd have found his way back to Heinola by now, even on foot?

The photographer thought he'd better ring the journalist's wife in Helsinki.

She muttered sleepily that there'd been no sign of Vatanen and, when she realized the caller was drunk, banged the receiver down. When the photographer tried the same number again, there was no reply. Clearly, Vatanen's wife had unplugged the telephone.

In the early hours, the photographer called for a taxi. He'd decided to go back to the site and see if Vatanen was still there. The taxi-driver asked his drunken client where it was he wished to go.

'Just drive along this road, nowhere in particular. I'll tell you where to stop.'

The driver glanced back. They were driving out of town through the night forest and not going anywhere in particular apparently. Furtively, he transferred a pistol from the glove compartment on to the seat between his legs. Uneasily, he studied the client.

At the top of a rise, the client said: 'Stop here.'

The driver eased the pistol into his hand. The drunk, however, got out of the car pacifically, and began shouting at the forest: 'Vatanen! Vatanen!'

The night forest didn't return even an echo.

'Vatanen! Hey, Vatanen! Are you there?'

He took off his shoes, rolled his trousers up to his knees, and set off into the forest, barefoot. Soon he'd vanished in the darkness. He could be heard yelling for Vatanen among the trees.

You get them all! the driver thought.

After about half an hour's shindy in the dark forest, the client returned to the road. Asking for a rag, he wiped his muddy shanks and put his shoes on his bare feet; the socks seemed to be in his jacket pocket. They drove back to Heinola.

'You've lost some Vatanen, have you?'

'Right. Left him there on the hill, in the evening. Not a whiff of him there now.'

'Didn't see anything myself, either,' the driver said sympathetically.

Next morning, the photographer woke up in the hotel at about eleven. A nasty hangover was splitting his head, and he felt sick. He remembered Vatanen's disappearance. Must get on to Vatanen's wife at her job . . . he thought.

'He went off after a hare,' he told her. 'On this hill. Then never came back. Of course I kept shouting, but not a squeak from him.

So I left him there. Probably he wanted to stay there.'

To this, the wife said: 'Was he drunk?'

'No.'

'So where is he, then? The man can't just disappear like that.'

'He did just disappear like that. Not turned up there yet, I suppose?'

'No, definitely not. God, that man'll drive me round the bend. Let him sort this out on his own. The thing is, he's got to get back home straight away. Tell him that.'

'How can I tell him anything? I don't even know where he is.'

'Well, ferret him out. Get him to ring me at work, straight away. And tell him this is the last time he goes on the loose. Listen, I've a customer, I've got to go. Tell him to ring me. Bye.'

The photographer rang the newspaper office.

'Yes . . . and one other thing: Vatanen's disappeared.'

'Oh. Where's he off to this time?' the editor asked.

The photographer told him the story.

'He'll turn up in his own good time, won't he? Anyway, this story of yours isn't so drastic we can't shelve it a day or two. We'll run it when he gets back.'

'But what if he's had an accident?'

The editor soothed him down: 'Just get back here yourself. What d'you suppose *could* have happened to him? And, anyway, it's *his* business.'

'Should I tell the police?'

'Tell his wife, if you like. Does she know?'

'She knows, but she's not bothering much.'

'Well, it's not particularly our problem either.'

2 Statement of Account

Early next morning Vatanen woke up to birdsong in a sweet-smelling hayloft. The hare was lying in his armpit, apparently following the flitting of the swallows under the barn's ridgepiece – perhaps still building their nest there, or maybe feeding chicks already, judging by their busy dipping into the barn and out again.

The sun was gleaming through the gaps in the barn's warped old beams, and the piled-up hay was a warm bed. Lost in thought, Vatanen lolled in the hay for an hour or so before he got up and went out with the hare in his arms.

There was an old meadow, full of wild flowers, and a brook murmuring beyond it. Vatanen put the hare down by the brook, stripped off and took a cold dip. A tight shoal of tiny fish, swimming upstream, took fright at the slightest movement, invariably forgetting their fear the next moment.

Vatanen's thoughts turned to his wife in Helsinki. He began to feel depressed.

He didn't like his wife. There was something not very nice about her: she'd been unpleasant, or at any rate totally bound up with number one, all their married life. His wife had the habit of buying hideous clothes, naff and inconvenient: she never wore them for more than a while, because, once on, they soon lost their allure for her too. She'd certainly have discarded Vatanen as well, if she could have found someone new as easily as the clothes.

Early in the marriage his wife had single-mindedly set out to assemble a common domicile, a home. Their flat had become an extravagant farrago of shallow and meretricious interior-decoration tips from women's magazines. A pseudo-radicalism governed the design, with huge posters and clumsy modularized furniture. It was difficult to inhabit the rooms without injury; all the items were at odds. The home was distinctly reminiscent of Vatanen's marriage.

One spring, his wife became pregnant but quickly procured an abortion: a cot would have disturbed the harmony of the furnishings. But the real explanation came to Vatanen's notice after the abortion: the baby wasn't Vatanen's.

'Jealous of a dead foetus?' his wife spluttered when he brought the subject up. 'You can't be!'

Vatanen settled the leveret at the edge of the brook, so it could reach down for a drink. Its little hare-lip began lapping up fresh water: it was astonishingly thirsty for such a small creature. When it had drunk, it began tucking into the leafage on the bank. Its hind leg was obviously still painful.

Maybe I should head back to Helsinki? Vatanen was wondering. What would they be saying in the office?

But what an office, what a job! A weekly magazine, everlastingly creating a stir about supposed abuses, while craftily keeping mum on any fundamental ills of society. Week after week the rag's cover displayed the faces of no-goods – minxes, models, some rock-yodeller's latest offspring. When he was younger, Vatanen was pleased to have a reporter's job on a major journal, particularly so when he had the chance to interview some misrepresented person, ideally someone oppressed by the state. That way he felt he was doing some good: such and such a defect, at least, was getting an airing. But now, with the years, he no longer supposed he was achieving anything: he was merely doing the absolutely necessary, satisfied if he personally was not contributing any misconceptions. His colleagues were in the same mould: frustrated at work, cynical in consequence. No need for marketing experts to tell journalists like these what stories the publisher expected. The stories were churned out. The magazine succeeded, but not by transmitting information – by diluting it, muffling its significance, cooking it into chatty entertainment. What a profession!

Vatanen was on a reasonably good salary, but even so he was always in financial difficulties. His flat cost hundreds a month: rents in Helsinki were so high. Because of the rent, he'd never be in a position to buy his own place. He had managed to get himself a boat, but for that too he was in debt. Apart from sailing, Vatanen

had no particular pastimes. His wife sometimes suggested going to
the theatre, but he'd no wish to go out with her: he'd had enough
of her voice at home.

Vatanen sighed.

The summer morning was getting brighter and brighter, but his
gloomy thoughts were getting darker and darker. Not till the hare
had eaten and Vatanen had put it in his pocket did the wretched
thoughts leave him. Purposefully, he set off west, the direction he'd
taken the evening before, shunning the road. The forest murmur
gladdened him. He hummed a couple of snatches. The hare's ears
poked out of his jacket pocket.

After an hour or two Vatanen came to a village. Walking along
the main street, he found a red kiosk. A girl was bustling round it,
just about to open her little business, apparently.

He went over to the kiosk, said a good-morning and sat down
on the bench. The girl opened the shutters, went in the kiosk, slid
aside a glass partition, and said: 'We're open now. Can I help
you?'

Vatanen bought some cigarettes and a bottle of lemonade. The
girl studied him carefully and then said: 'You're not a criminal,
are you?'

'No . . . do I scare you?'

'No, that's not it. You came out of the forest, you see.'

Vatanen took the hare out of his pocket and let it bumble around
on the kiosk bench.

'Hey, a bunny!' the girl whooped.

'Not a bunny, it's a hare. I found it.'

'Aw, poor thing! It's got a sore leg. I'll get it some carrots.'

She left her kiosk and ran into a house nearby. Soon she was
back with a bunch of last season's carrots. She washed the soil off
with a dash of lemonade and eagerly offered them to the hare, but
it didn't eat. That made her a little disappointed.

'He doesn't seem to take to them.'

'He's a bit sick. You don't have a vet in the village, do you?'

'Oh, yes, there's Mattila. He's not from round here, of course –
from Helsinki. Always here in the summers, off in the winters. His
villa's over there, by the lake-shore. Climb on the roof, and I'll
show you which it is.'

Vatanen climbed on the kiosk roof, and from down below the
girl told him which way to look, and what colour the villa was.

Vatanen looked towards where she said and spotted the villa. Then he climbed down with the girl's hands supporting his bottom.

The vet gave the hare a small injection and carefully bandaged its hind leg.

'It's had a shock. The paw will heal all right. If you take it to town, get it some fresh lettuce. It'll eat that. Don't forget to rinse the lettuce well, or it might get the squitters. For drinking, nothing but fresh water.'

When Vatanen got back to the kiosk, several men were sitting there with time on their hands. The girl introduced Vatanen: 'Here he is, the man with the hare.'

The men were drinking lager. They were fascinated by the hare and asked a lot of questions. They tried to reckon how old it might be. One of them related how, whenever he was going haymaking, he first went round the hayfields shouting, so any leverets hidden there would run away.

'Otherwise the blades'll get 'em. One summer there were three. One had its ears cut off, another lost its back legs, another was cut in two. The summers I've chased 'em off first, not one got caught in the machine.'

The village was so agreeable, Vatanen stayed on there several days, occupying an attic in one of the houses.

3 Arrangements

Vatanen took the bus for Heinola: even in an agreeable village, one can't hang around doing nothing for ever.

He sat on the back seat of the bus, with the hare in a basket. Several countrymen were sitting at the back, so they could smoke. When they spotted the hare, they started building a conversation round it. There were, it was soon established, more leverets than usual this summer. They tried to guess: was it a doe or a buck? Did he intend to slaughter and eat the hare when it was fully grown? No, he had no such intention, he said. That led to a general consensus: no one would kill his own dog; and it was sometimes easier to get attached to an animal than a person.

Vatanen took a room in a hotel, washed and went downstairs to eat. It was midday, the restaurant completely deserted. Vatanen sat the hare on the chair next to him.

The head waiter observed it, menu in hand: 'Strictly speaking, animals are not allowed in the restaurant.'

'It's not dangerous.'

Vatanen ordered lunch for himself, and for the hare a fresh lettuce, grated carrot and pure water. The head waiter gave a long look when Vatanen put the hare on the table to eat the lettuce out of the dish, but he didn't go so far as to forbid it.

After the meal Vatanen rang his wife on the hall telephone.

'So it's you, is it?' she cried in a fury. 'Where on earth are you? Get back here at once!'

'I've been thinking, I may not come back at all.'

'Oh, that's what you've been thinking, is it? You've gone completely round the bend. Now you *have* to come home. This lark'll get you fired too, that's for certain. And besides, Antero and Kerttu are coming round tonight. What am I going to say to them?'

'Say I've scarpered. Then at least you won't have to lie.'

'How can I tell them something like that! What'll they think? If this is looking for a divorce, it won't work, I can tell you! I'm not letting you off that way when you've ruined my life – eight years down the drain because of you! Daft I was to take you!'

She began to cry.

'Cry quicker, or the call'll get too expensive.'

'If you don't come back here at once I'll get the police. That'll teach you to stay at home!'

'It's hardly a case for the police.'

'Believe me, I'll phone up Antti Ruuhonen straight away. That'll show you I've got company.'

Vatanen put the receiver down.

Then he rang his friend Yrjö.

'Listen, Yrjö. I'm willing to sell you the boat.'

'You don't mean it! Where are you ringing from?'

'I'm in the country, Heinola. I'm not planning to come back to Helsinki for the moment, and I need some dosh. Do you still want it?'

'Definitely. How much? Seven grand was it?'

'OK, let's say that. You can get the keys from the office. Bottom left-hand drawer of my desk – two keys on a blue plastic ring. Ask Leena. You know her, she can give you them. Say I said so. Do you have the ready?'

'Yes, I do. Are you including the berth?'

'Yes, that's included. Do it this way: go straight to my bank and pay off the rest of my loan.' Vatanen gave him his account number. 'Then go to my wife. Give her two and a half thousand. Then send the remaining three thousand two hundred express to the bank in Heinola – same bank. Is that all right?'

'And your charts come in the deal as well?'

'They do. They're at home, you'll get them off my wife. Listen. Don't land that boat on a rock? Take it easy for starters and you'll not get in a twist.'

'Tell me, how do you have the heart to sell it? Have you lost your nerve?'

'You could say that.'

The following day Vatanen was off to the Heinola bank, carrying his hare. His step was light, his manner carefree, as might be expected.

Much has been said about the sixth sense, and the closer he got to the bank, the more distinctly he began to feel that matters weren't quite as they should be. He was already on his guard when he got to the bank, though he had no idea what was awaiting him. He supposed that even a few days of freedom had sharpened his senses, an amusing thought that made him smile as he entered the bank.

His intuition had been right.

In the entrance hall, back to the door, sat his wife. His heart leaped, anger and fear flooded his body. Even the hare jumped.

He dashed out again. He ran along the street as fast as his legs would carry him. Oncomers stopped in astonishment to see a man bolting out of a bank with a basket and two small hare's ears poking out of it. He tore to the end of the block, nipped down a side-street, found a little tavern door, and slipped straight into the restaurant. He was out of breath.

'If I'm not mistaken, sir, you're Mr Vatanen,' the head waiter said, looking at the hare as if he recognized it. 'You're expected.'

At the other end of the restaurant sat the photographer and the chief editor. They were drinking beer together and hadn't noticed Vatanen. The head waiter explained that the gentlemen had asked him to direct a person looking like Mr Vatanen to their table, and that he might have a hare with him.

Again Vatanen had been trapped.

He slipped out again, sneaked back to his hotel and tried to think. What had gone wrong with his arrangements? Of course, bloody Yrjö was at the back of it.

He rang Yrjö, Yrjö, the nitwit, had told Vatanen's wife where he was sending the remainder of the money. The rest could be imagined: his wife had ganged up with the office, and they'd come to Heinola to grab him. She was sitting in the bank now, waiting for him to collect his cash.

The money had been sent to the bank, but how could he get hold of it without a scene? It needed thinking out.

He hit on it. He rang down to the receptionist and asked her to make out his bill, but adding that three people would soon be coming to meet him in his room, a woman and two men. Then he wrote a few words on the hotel writing-paper, and left the note on the table. This done, he looked up the number of the restaurant where he'd just been dancing like a cat on hot bricks, grabbed the telephone and rang; the head waiter replied.

'Vatanen speaking. Could you get me one or other of the two men who're expecting me?'

'Is that Vatanen?' came a voice shortly. It was the editor.

'Speaking. Morning.'

'You've had it. Guess what: your old woman's sitting in the bank, and we're right here. Get round here fast, and then we can all be off back to Helsinki. Time this stopped.'

'Listen, I can't get there this minute. Come here, all three of you, to my hotel room. It's 312. I've got to make these two long-distance calls. Pick my wife up from the bank, and we'll sort the whole thing out together, the four of us.'

'Right, OK. We'll be round. Stay where you are, though!'

'Of course. Bye.'

This said, Vatanen rushed out into the lift with the hare and paid the receptionist for the room and his calls. He told her, though, that he'd like her to let in three people who were coming to meet him. Still on the trot, he slipped out into the street.

He took a side-street route to the bank. Peeping through the glass doors, he saw his wife had not gone, dammit! He retreated and lurked round the corner.

Soon two men emerged from the tavern nearby, the editor and the photographer. They entered the bank. Shortly they appeared again, accompanied by Vatanen's wife. All three set off in the direction of the hotel. Vatanen could hear his wife: 'I told you this was the only way we'd get him, didn't I?'

When the three were out of sight, Vatanen went quietly into the bank, approached the cashier, and produced his identification. Looking at his name on the card, the cashier said: 'Your wife was here a minute ago, looking for you. She's just left.'

'Yes, I know. I'll catch up with her in a moment.'

There had been quite a hefty express charge on Vatanen's money, but he'd been left with the equivalent of just over three thousand pounds. He signed for it and collected the notes: quite a bit to count. The hare crouched on the glass-plated counter. The women of the bank had all dropped what they were doing and gathered round to admire the handsome creature; they were eager to stroke it.

'But please don't touch the hind paw, it's broken,' Vatanen warned, benignly.

'Oh, it's adorable,' they said. The bank was filled with a heart-warming atmosphere of joy.

When he finally managed to get away, Vatanen hastened to the taxi-rank, climbed into a big black limousine and said: 'Mikkeli, please – and fast as you can.'

In Vatanen's hotel room a vehement discussion was in progress. It was caused by the note Vatanen had left on the table. It read: *Leave me in peace. Vatanen.*

4 Grasses

Mikkeli in sunshine, total liberty: Vatanen was sitting on a bench in Central Park. The hare was nosing about in the grass for something to eat. On their way from the bus station, four gipsy women dressed in bright, multicoloured skirts stopped to have a look at the hare and chat with Vatanen. They were in high spirits and wanted to buy the hare.

They knew where the South Savo Game Preservation Office was and directed him. One of them was very insistent on telling Vatanen's fortune. 'A great turning-point in your life,' she explained: he'd been under great pressure and had made a big decision. His fate line, down the middle of his hand, was now showing a fabulous future ahead; many journeys in view, no need for anxiety. When Vatanen tried to give her money, she refused.

'Goodness gracious, darling, I don't need money in the summer.'

The Game Preservation Office had a note on the door, announcing that the game warden, U. Kärkkäinen, was available at his home. Vatanen took a taxi to the address. In the yard a big dog set off barking, and when it scented the hare it took to howling. Vatanen didn't want to risk going farther.

A big-set, youngish man came out to control the dog, and Vatanen was able to go in. Then the game warden invited his visitor to sit down and asked how he could help.

'I want to know the kind of things an animal of this sort eats,' Vatanen began, and he pulled the hare out of the basket on to the table between them. 'A vet in Heinola said lettuce, but it's not always convenient, and the creature doesn't seem to go for grass.'

Kärkkäinen looked at the leveret with expert interest.
'A buck. Hardly even a month old, I'd say. Is this a pet, or what?
That's strictly forbidden, you know, by the game-protection laws.'
'Yes, but it'd have died, you see, no question. Its leg was broken.'
'So I see. But we'd better make it legal. I'll write you an official
permit. Then you can hold on to it as a fostered pet.'
He began to type a few lines on a sheet of paper; he added an
official stamp and signed his name at the bottom. It read:

PERMIT TO RETAIN A WILD ANIMAL
It is herewith certified that Kaarlo Vatanen, the possessor of
this permit, is officially authorized to take care of and rear a
wild forest hare, on the grounds that the permit-holder took
charge of the leveret when injured in its left hind leg and
consequently at risk of death.
U.Kärkkäinen, Game Warden
South Savo Game Preservation Office, Mikkeli

'Feed it early clover. You'll find a lot of that almost anywhere
now. And for drinking, give it pure water; no point in forcing
milk on it. Besides clover, fresh grass may do, and barley after-
math . . . bonnet grass it likes, and meadow vetchling. In fact, it
likes all the vetches, and alsike is something it likes too. In the
winter, you'd best give it the cambium of deciduous trees, and
deep-frozen bilberry twigs as well, if you're keeping it in town.'
'What sort of a plant is meadow vetchling? I don't know it.'
'But the vetches you do know?'
'I think I do. They belong to the pea family, don't they? They've
got the same sort of clinging tendrils as peas.'
'Meadow vetchling's very like vetch. It's got yellow flowers –
they're the easiest way to know it. I'll draw a picture of it for
you, then you'll be able to spot it.'
Kärkkäinen took out a large sheet of paper and began to draw
plants with a lead pencil. A skilful drawer he was not. The pencil
advanced across the paper in a hefty fist. The lead dug deep into
the paper, and a couple of times the lead snapped. After a long
effort, an image began to form.
Vatanen was peeping at the developing image with keen interest.
Kärkkäinen drew the sheet aside, showing a desire to bring his
creative work to a conclusion undisturbed.

'And then there are these little yellow flowers . . . dammit. There should be some yellow, to give you a better idea. I'll go and get my son's water-colours.'

Kärkkäinen fetched some water and began colouring a thickset picture of a plant, He coloured the stems and the leaves green, carefully cleaning the brush before he turned to colouring the flowers yellow.

'This paper's a little on the thin side. The colour spreads.'

When the flowers were tinted yellow, Kärkkäinen pushed his painting materials to one side and blew on the painting to dry it. He took a long look at his work, holding it well away, to assess the result.

'Don't know if this picture's going to be much use to you after all, but roughly this is how the plant looks. It's something a hare'll gladly take to. Those tendrils have come out a bit thick. Mentally you'll have to thin them down a bit when you're out looking for the real thing. Have you got a brief-case for this, so there's no need to fold it?'

Vatanen shook his head. Kärkkäinen gave him a big grey envelope, large enough to take the picture unfolded.

Vatanen thanked him for all his advice. The game warden smiled, slightly embarrassed but pleased. In the yard, the men shook hands warmly.

The taxi-driver had been waiting outside for half an hour. Vatanen asked him to drive to the outskirts of the town, to some place where there'd be luxuriant greenery. They found a suitable spot without too much trouble: a largish spinney of birches, overgrown with dandelions on the roadside.

The taxi-driver asked if he could get out and help to pick the flowers: time tended to drag, sitting alone in a hot car.

That was just fine.

Vatanen handed him Kärkkäinen's water-colour. It wasn't long before the taxi-driver, ferreting about in the spinney, gave a whoop: he'd found some meadow vetchling. Several others of the game warden's recommendations were growing nearby too.

'I've always been fascinated by plants,' the taxi-driver confessed to Vatanen.

After an hour the men had each gathered an armful of suitable eatables. The hare gobbled them eagerly. In the meantime the driver went off to fetch some water from the hydrant. He brought it in a hub-cap, first giving the cap a good rinse under the tap. The hare took long draughts from the hub-cap, and the taxi-driver shared the rest with Vatanen. When the water was finished, the driver slammed the hub-cap back on his front wheel.

'Why not take these grasses round to my place? They can stay in the hall cupboard while you're looking for a hotel or something.'

Back in town, they drove to the taximan's block of flats and into the yard. They gathered up their armfuls of plants and took the lift to the fourth floor. The door of the flat was opened by a diffident woman who looked a little astonished to see her husband and another man standing there with armfuls of sweet-smelling plants.

'Helvi, these plants belong to my passenger. We're going to put them in the cupboard till he needs them.'

'Mercy on us,' she groaned. 'How'll they all fit in?' But she stopped when she saw the look of annoyance on her husband's face.

Vatanen paid the fare. Before leaving, he thanked the driver yet again.

The taximan said: 'Just give me a ring, and I'll bring the grasses over.'

5 Arrest

By mid-June Vatanen's travels had landed him on the road to Nurmes. It was raining, he was cold.

He'd jumped out of the coach from Kuopio, which was now off to Nurmes. And here he was, on a rainy road, getting soaked because of a snap decision. The village of Nilsiä was miles off.

The hare's hind leg had mended, and, by now, it was almost fully grown. Luckily, it still fitted in the basket.

But, anyway, round the corner he found a house: a bungalow with attic space – a prosperous-looking set-up. Might as well call, Vatanen decided, and see if a night's lodging is available. A woman in a raincoat was scraping away at the garden, hands black with soil: an older woman – and a picture of his wife flashed through his mind. Something in this woman reminded him of her.

'Good-evening.'

She rose from her crouch, gazed at the newcomer, and then at the wet hare, which was hopping at Vatanen's feet.

'My name's Vatanen. I've just come from Kuopio, and I got out here by mistake. I should have gone on to Nilsiä. It's raining quite a bit, as one might expect round here, I suppose.'

The woman was still staring at the hare.

'What on earth is that?'

'Just a hare. From near Heinola. I adopted him as a sort of travelling companion . . . we've been doing the trip together.'

'So what's your business? she asked suspiciously.

'No special business, actually – I'm just going the rounds, visiting various places with the hare, passing the time . . . and, as I said, I got out of the coach, and I'm already getting rather weary.

I suppose there's no chance of your putting me up for the night?'

'I'll have to ask Aarno.'

She went inside. The hare was hungry and started nibbling the plants in the garden. Vatanen stopped it, and finally picked it up in his arms.

A man appeared at the front door, small, middle-aged, slightly balding. 'Clear off,' he said. 'You can't stay here. On your way now.'

Vatanen felt a little vexed. He asked the man if he'd at least ring for a taxi.

The man repeated his injunction to clear off, looking slightly scared now. Vatanen went over to the front door to sort out the matter, but the man slipped inside, slamming the door in his face. Funny lot! Vatanen thought.

'Ring now, he's completely crackers,' came the woman's voice through the window.

Vatanen assumed they were ringing for a taxi.

'Hello, Laurila speaking. Get down here fast, quick as you can. He's at the door, tried to break in, completely round the bend. Got a hare with him.'

The call ended. Vatanen tried the front door: locked. The rain was coming down. An angry face appeared at the window, yelling 'Stop hacking at the door . . . I've got a weapon.'

Vatanen went and sat on the garden swing – it had an awning. The woman called from the window: 'Don't you try to get in!'

After a while a black police car turned into the drive. Two uniformed constables emerged from the car and approached Vatanen. The people of the house now appeared at their door, pointing at Vatanen, and saying: 'Take him away, he's the one.'

'Right, then,' the constables said. 'What've you been up to?'

'I asked them to ring for a taxi, but they've rung for you instead.'

'And am I right in thinking you've got a hare with you?'

Vatanen opened the lid of the basket: the hare had just crept into it, out of the rain. The hare peered nervously out of the basket, looking somehow guilty.

The constables gave each other a look, nodded, and one of them said: 'Right, sir; better come along with us. Hand over that basket.'

6 The District Superintendent

The police sat in front, with the hare. Vatanen was at the back, alone. At first they travelled in silence, but just before they reached the village, the constable holding the basket said: 'Do you mind if I have a look?'

'Certainly, but don't lift him up by the ears.'

The constable opened the basket and looked at the hare, which stretched its head over the top. The constable at the wheel craned round to look. He changed down and slowed up to see better.

'This year's,' the driver said. 'Could be a March hare, perhaps?'

'Hardly. A week or two ago he was still very small. Probably born in June.'

'It's a buck,' the other constable said.

They arrived at the village of Nilsiä, and the car drove into the police station forecourt. The basket lid was put on again. Vatanen was taken inside.

The constable on duty was sitting there looking sleepy, his uniform shirt unbuttoned. He visibly perked up on seeing company.

Vatanen was offered a chair. He dug some cigarettes out of his pocket and offered them to the police. They glanced at each other first and then each took a cigarette. The telephone rang, the duty officer replied.

'Nilsiä police station, Heikkinen speaking. Ah. All right, we'll pick him up tomorrow. Oh, quiet enough, just one case this evening.'

The duty officer regarded Vatanen as if estimating what sort of case this was.

'We had a call about him – Laurila it was. Evidently attempted breaking and entry. Seems decent enough. Just brought in. Bye now.'

He put the receiver down.

'Social welfare officer. We'll have to go and pick up Hanninen tomorrow – otherwise he won't move, apparently.'

The duty officer gave Vatanen an interrogative look. He arranged a few papers on his desk, and then summoned a more official tone.

'Yes . . . this business. May I see your papers?'

Vatanen gave him his wallet. The officer took out the identification papers and a wad of banknotes. The others came over to see the contents. The duty officer studied the identification papers and then began counting the money. It took quite a while; the duty officer's level voice echoed in the room as he went on with his work. It was like reckoning up the final results of the presidential elections.

He whistled. 'Two thousand, seven hundred and eight quid.'

There was a silence.

Then Vatanen explained: 'I sold my boat.'

'You don't happen to have the receipt with you?'

Vatanen had to admit he didn't.

'Never had a wad like that in my wallet in all my life,' one of the arresting constables said.

'Me neither,' said the other, darkly.

'Are you the Vatanen who writes for them weeklies?' the duty officer asked.

Vatanen nodded.

'So what's your business in these parts, then? Some writing job, is it? Seeing you've got that hare with you?'

No, Vatanen said. He wasn't on an assignment. Where, he asked, could he spend the night? He was getting more than a bit tired.

'We've got this charge preferred against you, though. Dr Laurila's. He's the local doctor. He's told us to detain you. That's all I have to go on.'

Vatanen said he didn't see how some Laurila could simply take it on himself to have whomever he liked detained.

'But in any case it's our duty to make some enquiries, seeing you've got all that cash on your person. And what's the meaning of this hare? The local doctor claims you attempted to break in, coerced him to ring for a taxi . . . *and* threateningly demanded overnight accommodation. Quite enough there to keep you in custody – though not implying any very big issue, of course. If only you'd say what your business here is.'

Vatanen explained that he had left his home and his job, that he was in fact on a walk-out. He hadn't yet managed to decide what he would do next. In the meantime he was having a look round this part of the country.

'I'd best get on to the lads in Kuopio,' the duty officer decided and rang a number. 'Hello, Heikkinen here, from Nilsiä. Evening. We've got an odd case here . . . to start with, he's toting a tame hare around. A journalist he is. Criminal charges were phoned in – been disturbing the peace, trying to force entry into a house for the night . . . yes, and in his wallet he's got two thousand seven hundred-odd in notes. He seems all there, though. That's not why I'm ringing – it's what to do with him? He wants to be off . . . yes, I can certainly put it in writing as well. . . . He says he's not doing anything in particular – just having a look around these parts with his hare. Not drunk either – no, decent-looking enough. Yes. But it could cause a hassle. . . . You don't say. . . . Right, well, we'd better hang on to him then, I suppose. . . . So, thanks a lot – raining, it is, quite a downpour here, been coming down the whole day. . . . Cheers.

'The lads in Kuopio say they at any rate'd keep you inside the first night. You're a vagrant, and in possession of all that cash – added to which there's the criminal charge. So, do you accept all that?'

'Can't you ring the district superintendent? Surely you're not under the authority of Kuopio.'

'I'd have rung him from the start, but the superintendent's out fishing at this moment in time. He won't be back till tennish, if then. I'm unfortunately the most senior officer here. Kuopio advised not turning you loose in any circumstances. Anyway, where would you go now, on a wet night like this?'

'But where are you going to put this hare?' Vatanen added, with a touch of malice.

Attention again focused on the hare, whose basket had been moved from table to floor during the counting. From down there, the leveret was peacefully following the progress of the interrogation. It saw a new problem dawning for the police.

'Hmm . . . where to put that hare, then . . . so what if we confiscate it, for the state – and let it out in the forest? It'd surely manage there well enough.'

Vatanen produced the licence he'd obtained in Mikkeli.

'I have an official permit to keep this animal in my care. It cannot be confiscated, or illegally turned loose – deprived of my protection, in other words. You can't put it in a cell either. A cell's too unsanitary a place for a sensitive wild animal. It could perish.'

'I could take it home for the night,' one of the younger constables offered.

But Vatanen had an objection: 'Only if you're trained in the management of wild rodents and possess an appropriate hutch. In addition, the animal definitely requires special foods – meadow vetchling, and many other special herbs. Otherwise it could die of food poisoning. If anything happened to the hare, you'd be liable, and animals of this quality are costly.'

The hare was following the interchange; it appeared to nod during Vatanen's words.

'A fine mess,' the duty officer exploded. 'You'd better be off. Get back here tomorrow, for interrogation. Ten sharp. And take that hare with you.'

'Hold on,' the young constables warned. 'What'll Laurila say when he hears that? And what do we know about this chap? Look at that money. Yet he hasn't even got a car. Where's he from? Is he really Vatanen, in fact?'

'Yes. . . . Hm. So don't go yet. Have to think. Bit of a bind, the super's out fishing. Anyone got a fag?'

Vatanen offered more cigarettes. Again they smoked. Nothing was said for quite a while.

Finally, the younger constable said to Vatanen: 'Don't get us wrong. We've nothing against you personally, you know, nothing at all, but we have our regulations, for ourselves too, the police. Without that hare, for example, everything'd be so much simpler. Look at it from our point of view. For all we know, you might be a murderer. Could have done someone in before you left Helsinki . . . gone off your head, perhaps, wandering aimlessly around here. In fact, you *are* wandering aimlessly . . . you might be a danger to the whole community.'

'Let's not go over the top,' the duty officer said. 'No one's talking about murder.'

'But we could be, in theory. I don't say we are, but we could easily be.'

'Just as easily I could be a murderer myself,' the duty officer snorted. He stubbed out his cigarette, gave the hare an angry stare, and then: 'Let's do it this way. Stay here regardless – in this duty room if you like . . . till I can ring up the superintendent. That'll be in a couple of hours or so. Then we'll have it all sorted out. Meanwhile take a nap on that bunk, if you're tired. If you like, we'll have some coffee. What's all the hurry? How does that sound?'

Vatanen accepted the offer.

The hare, in its basket, was put on a night-duty bed at the rear of the room. Vatanen asked if he could have a look at the sort of cell accommodation there was at Nilsiä police station. The duty officer willingly got up to show him. The whole company trooped to the lock-up, and the duty officer opened one of the doors and explained: 'Nothing special, these – mostly we only get drunks. We do get people from Tahkavuori sometimes. We've had some quite important people inside too.'

There were two adjoining cells: modest rooms. The windows, frosted wired glass, had no bars. Screwed to the wall there was a tubular bed, a lidless WC, and a chair, also fastened immovably. A lamp without a lampshade dangled from the ceiling.

'They generally smash that lamp in their rage, and so they get to sit in the dark. Should put a steel frame round it – the tallest can jump that high.'

The policemen made some coffee. Vatanen went to lie down on the duty-room bed. The officers chatted about Vatanen's case in subdued tones, thinking he was asleep. He overheard the men's assessment of Laurila. All in all, they thought it a pretty out-of-the-way case: best to proceed cautiously at the start. Vatanen dozed off.

Later, about ten, the duty officer woke Vatanen. The superintendent had been contacted and was on his way. Vatanen rubbed his eyes, looked at the basket by his feet and saw it was empty.

'The lads are out in the forecourt with it. We saw it didn't run off, and we thought it could be hungry, so we procured some of that meadow vetchling you mentioned. Jolly good feed it's had, in fact.'

The younger constables re-entered with the hare. They let it go hopping round the floor, leaving little pills everywhere. The officers kicked the droppings into the corners but, finding that not very satisfactory, they grabbed a rag off the coffee-table and whisked the droppings up against the wall.

A little yellow car drove into the forecourt. The superintendent came in. He noticed the hare on the floor, showed no surprise, offered his hand to Vatanen and announced his name: 'Savolainen.'

The duty officer put the whole case to him. The superintendent was a youngish man, probably a recent graduate in jurisprudence, in the sticks as a stage in his career. He certainly looked professional enough as he listened to the evidence.

'The lads in Kuopio told you to lock him up?'

'That's what they recommended, but we didn't go ahead till we heard from you.'

'You did right. I know Laurila.'

The superintendent examined Vatanen's papers and returned his money to him. 'I'll give the doctor a ring,' he said and picked up the telephone.

'District Superintendent Savolainen here. Good-evening. You have, I understand, brought criminal charges against a certain person. Yes, quite. However, the situation is this: your report has no foundation. This is the conclusion we've arrived at in the course of our investigations. It's important that you come here at once to clear the matter up. Tomorrow won't do, by any means. This will be a very difficult situation for you unless somehow or other you can sort the matter out. If the person concerned presses charges, I don't know what I, as a police officer, can do about it. In any case, the person has been held here on your responsibility and could prefer charges of false accusation against you. He's been compelled to endure a considerable time here at the police station. When you arrive, you won't find me here, but you can explain yourself to the duty officer, who will be responsible for interrogating you. Goodbye.'

The superintendent grinned. To Heikkinen he said: 'Sound out Laurila. Question him about this and that. Force him to think up suitable answers. Ask whatever you like – you could even take his fingerprints. When you've finished, tell him he can go. Say that neither the public prosecutor nor I will pursue charges unless the person concerned considers it appropriate. Well, you know the form. Yes, and Vatanen, where are you going for the night? I'm off back to the lake till morning. I put some nets out. Why not come along with me for the night? You can bring that hare of yours. It's a little log cabin by the lake – just a fishing sauna. The hare can run wild there, and you can sleep in peace.'

The constables accompanied Vatanen, the superintendent and the hare to the station forecourt.

The duty officer said to the superintendent: 'Right from the start, sir, I saw this Mr Vatanen was a respectable person.'

7 The President

The superintendent's little fishing cabin and sauna were a few yards from a lake in the forest. They were a pile of old logs on quaking bogland, reached by duckboard.

'Inside you'll find my fishing crony, quite a character, rather special. Retired now, used to be the Kiuruvesi superintendent of police. Name of Hannikainen.'

When they got to the cabin, Hannikainen was sitting with his back to the door: he was grilling fish on the heating-stove in the corner, its iron doors open for the job. He pushed the gridiron to one side and shook hands, then offered the new arrivals hot fish on pieces of greaseproof paper. By now Vatanen was truly hungry. They gave the hare some fresh grass and water.

The two others went out, and Vatanen collapsed on to a bunk. Half asleep, he felt the hare hopping on to the bunk by his feet, shuffling into a comfortable position, and settling down for the night too.

Sleepily, in the early hours, Vatanen heard the men returning from the lake and chatting outside in low tones before turning in. The superintendent went into the sauna to bunk down on the boards; Hannikainen stretched on a bunk in the cabin. The hare raised its head but soon went back to sleep.

In the morning Vatanen woke fresh and alert. It was eight o'clock. Hannikainen's bunk was empty. The fishermen had probably only just risen and were getting a scratch fire going outside. A coffee-kettle dangled from the bar above the fire, and Hannikainen shook some butter pretzels out of a plastic bag. Waders were crying from the shore. A morning mist lay over the water, and a bright day was on the way.

After coffee, the superintendent set off for the village to take up his duties. The sound of his car faded down the forest road and drifted out of earshot.

Hannikainen went into the cabin and came out with some lard, which he sliced into the frying-pan on the fire. The fat sizzled, and he tipped a pound tin of beef and pork into it. The fry-up was soon ready. Hannikainen cut some long slices from a large loaf of rye bread, put the burning-hot fried meat on them, and presented some to Vatanen. It was delicious. In Helsinki Vatanen usually had difficulty in coping with breakfast, but now the food tasted marvellous.

Hannikainen lent Vatanen the superintendent's fishing gear, rubber boots and a fishing smock. Vatanen's own shoes and suit were left hanging on a nail in the cabin. Probably they are there to this day.

The men loafed around the cabin all day, fishing, making fish soup, lolling in the sun, looking at the sedgy lake. In the evening Hannikainen took a bottle of vodka from his rucksack, creaked the cork out and poured them a tot each.

Hannikainen was already getting on in years, knocking seventy, completely white-haired, tall, talkative. In the course of the day the men got to know each other. Vatanen related the what and wherefore of his journey. Hannikainen presented himself as a lonely widower spending his summers as the young superintendent's fishing companion. He was well informed on world affairs and inclined to ponder.

What, Vatanen wondered, was so unusual about Hannikainen? So far nothing to justify the superintendent's remark of the previous evening had appeared in Hannikainen's style of life, unless quiet summer fishing was coming to be considered unusual nowadays.

The answer to this question was on its way.

After the second tot of vodka Hannikainen began to lead the conversation round to government politics more seriously. He spoke of the responsibility of people in power, their influence and conduct, and revealed that, after retiring, he had begun to do some research into these concerns. In spite of a life spent as a police superintendent in a country parish, he was astonishingly well informed about the constitutions of the Western countries, the nuances of parliamentary law, and jurisdiction in the socialist countries. Vatanen listened with keen interest to Hannikainen's pronouncements on these major international questions, which constitutional lawyers often have to deal with in Finland too.

According to Hannikainen, Finland's constitution gave the president far too great a power of decision in state affairs. When Vatanen asked if he didn't think President Kekkonen had managed to make exemplary use of the powers devolved on him, Hannikainen replied: 'Over several years I've been making a close study of President Kekkonen ... and I'm coming to a most disturbing conclusion, disturbing to myself too. I don't mean I'm disturbed by his performance. I'm actually rather an enthusiastic supporter of his administration, but nevertheless.... All I'm doing is collecting information. I form comparisons, I sift, I make inferences. The result is extremely disturbing.'

'And what conclusions are you coming to?'

I've kept this affair a careful secret. No one but Savolainen knows, and a certain carpenter in Puumala. Neither of them will reveal the results of my investigations. You see – the conclusions my research has led to would, if published, have a nasty backlash. I might well lay myself open to the law, and at the very least I'd be made a laughing-stock.'

Hannikainen stared at Vatanen fixedly. His eyes froze.

'I'm getting on in years, and perhaps a little senile ... nevertheless, I'm not completely cracked. If you want to know what I've unearthed, you must give me your word that you won't use your knowledge against me, or against anyone else.'

Vatanen readily gave his word.

'It's a question of such moment that I can only beg you to give serious consideration to what I'm now going to tell you, and I insist that you never give me away.'

It was apparent that Hannikainen had a burning need to share his secret. He screwed the vodka cork back in the bottle, pushed the bottle into some moss and walked briskly to the cabin. Vatanen trailed after him.

Hanging on the cabin wall, between the window and the table, was a large, battered, brown suitcase. Vatanen had seen it the evening before but had paid no attention to it. Hannikainen lowered the case on to a bunk and snapped the catches open. The lid sprang upwards, revealing a store of tightly crammed documents and photographs.

'I haven't yet done the final sorting-out on this archive ... the research is still incomplete. But, in the main, it's all here. With the help of this, you'll reach a conclusion without much difficulty.'

Hannikainen started extracting documents from the suitcase: thick, typewritten leaflets, several books, and photographs all showing President Kekkonen in various settings. The books too concerned Kekkonen: they included editions of his speeches, Skytä's books on the president, and several other accounts, including a book of anecdotes. The documents included many graphics, which also, Vatanen saw, centred on Kekkonen.

Hannikainen produced several drawings on graph paper, showing careful longitudinal sections of human crania.

'Take a look at these,' Hannikainen said, showing two cranium pictures side by side in the pallid light of the window. 'Do you see the difference?'

At first glance, the pictures looked exactly alike, but on closer inspection they differed slightly in detail.

'This on the left shows Urho Kekkonen's cranium in 1945, just after the war, in fact. Then there is this one. It shows his cranium in 1972. I've prepared these drawings to show the changes with the years. My method has been to project outlines of ordinary photographs on to a screen – in different positions, naturally – and then transfer the outline of the cranium on to the graph paper. For Kekkonen this procedure offers no complications, owing to his complete baldness. The method is extremely long-drawn-out and demands unusual precision, but I have, in my view, achieved exceptionally good results. I'd say these are far more accurate crania mensurations than are normally achievable. Anything more accurate would have to come from a pathological laboratory, where the skull itself is at the researcher's disposal.'

Hannikainen selected another cranium picture.

'This is Kekkonen's cranium at the time of the formation of his third government. As you can perhaps see, it's precisely the same as the 1945 cranium. And here is the cranium of 1964, again the same.

'Now! Look at this: the cranium of 1969! What a difference! If you compare this, though, with the picture from 1972, you'll see that they again have a great deal in common.'

Hannikainen displayed his drawings excitedly, with burning eyes, smiling triumphantly. Vatanen studied the pictures and had to admit that Hannikainen's drawings were exactly as he said: the crania were different: the older crania differed from the more recent ones.

'The change occurred sometime during 1968, perhaps towards

the end of 1968, but in the first half of 1969 at the latest. I've not yet been able to pin down the time factor more precisely than this, but I'm continuing my studies, and I'm sure that I'll arrive at within a month or two of the precise date. In any case, I've already been able to prove, convincingly, that a change has taken place, and that the change is significant.'

Hannikainen paused. Then he said with emphasis: 'I tell you straight: these crania outlines are not diagrams of one and the same head. The difference is too marked, incontestably so. These old crania – from the time when Kekkonen was young, that is – are somewhat sharper on the crown, for example. In these recent pictures the cranium is flatter in formation: the crown is clearly rounder. And look at the jawbone. In the older pictures Kekkonen's jaw is noticeably withdrawn. In these recent pictures the jaw juts several millimetres further out than before, and at the same time the cheekbones are lower. This profile shows it best. Also the occiput has clear divergences, even if not so marked. In the old pictures the occiput is a little more flattened than in the recent ones. Look at that! When a person grows old, the occiput *never* becomes more salient – quite the reverse, I assure you.'

'What you're saying is that Kekkonen's head changed shape some time in the region of 1968?'

'I mean much more than that! What I've established is that around 1968 "The Old Kekkonen" either died or was murdered – or withdrew from government for some other reason – and his place was taken by someone else, almost exactly like the former Kekkonen, down to the voice.'

'But supposing Kekkonen became ill about that time, or had an accident that remoulded his skull?'

'Skull changes of this order would, if sickness were in question, or an accident, involve months of recuperation. My studies indicate that President Kekkonen was invariably too busy, all his life, to be absent from public exposure for longer than two uninterrupted weeks. And, in addition, I've been unable to find, in a single photograph, any evidence of scarring on the scalp. Warts, yes, but nothing indicating surgery in 1968.'

Hannikainen replaced the cranium pictures in the suitcase and displayed a large graph: a spreading curve annotated with numbers.

'This is the graph of Kekkonen's physical height. The numbers record his height since childhood . . . the figures from adolescence are not absolutely precise, but since Kekkonen's service as a sergeant they're completely watertight. Here is a photocopy of his ID card. See? Since his sergeant days Kekkonen has been 179 centimetres tall . . . he's the same height here, at the time of Paasikivi's funeral . . . and now look again! We come to the year 1968: the curve suddenly leaps a couple of centimetres. Kekkonen is in fact, all at once, nearly 181 centimetres. From then on the curve continues unchanged till this point, 1975, with no change in sight. A sudden increase in height in his latter days – something rather remarkable there, don't you think?'

Hannikainen thrust the table of the president's height aside. Somewhat frenziedly, he sought out a new table. It was a careful graph of Kekkonen's weight.

'Of course, these figures are nowhere near as conclusive, but they do add certain indices. Kekkonen's weight has changed very little since middle age. He has persisted in a certain annual cycle. In the autumn Kekkonen's weight goes up. He's sometimes as much as four and a half kilos heavier than in the spring. At the beginning of summer he's without exception at his lightest, returning again in the autumn to his maximum weight. I obtained these figures from the Occupational Health Institute in Helsinki, and so they're guaranteed accurate. But to follow the pattern decade by decade and compare the years with each other, I had to calculate Kekkonen's average weights for each year, and those are what this graph shows. Now you see, from 1956 right up to 1968 Kekkonen's average annual weight is 79 kilos. After 1968 it is 84 kilos. The five-kilo increase continues from 1968 to this day, absolutely steadily, apart from the seasonal cycle I referred to. All in all, only the first two presidential election years show an exception on the curve, a couple of kilos, and such a weight loss, even though diminishing the whole year's average, is quite natural and doesn't disturb the curve substantially.'

Hannikainen turned to additional evidence.

'I've drawn up a lexicon of Urho Kekkonen's vocabulary. Here too, we see the same divergence after 1968. Before 1968 Kekkonen's vocabulary was notably more limited than later. There's an increase of, by my reckoning, twelve hundred words in active use. The reason could of course be that after 1968 "The New Kekkonen", as I call him, was employing new speech-writers, but even so, an increase in vocabulary of that order is extremely indicative. In addition, I've established that a considerable alteration took place in Kekkonen's opinions after 1968. From 1969 Kekkonen's views were becoming increasingly progressive, quite as if Kekkonen had been rejuvenated, by ten years at least. His logic too was noticeably improving. I've analysed his performance here with extreme care, and, again, a clear change for the better occurs during 1968. Also, during 1969, Kekkonen was becoming somehow more boyish. He was getting up to tricks in public that he'd never have attempted before. Quite clearly, his sense of humour was developing, and he was becoming, as it were, much more tolerant towards the people of his country.'

Hannikainen shut his suitcase. He was now completely calm. There was no sign of his recent fervour. He seemed happy.

The two went out. A curlew's cry came from the lake. For a long time they were completely silent. Finally Hannikainen said: 'I'm sure you understand now that it would be unwise in the extreme to set about publishing researches like these.'

8 Forest Fire

The hare took to the lakeside life. It came along on Hannikainen and Vatanen's lake trips, hopped boldly into the punt with them, though it clearly feared water. It grew longer, plumper and stronger.

Hannikainen discoursed at length on President Kekkonen. The hare looked up at the men from the bottom of the punt, its head on one side. Its droppings rolled among the fish. In this manner, the days went by on the forest lake, and no one felt a need to go anywhere else.

One morning towards the end of July, the hare became restless. It lurked at the men's heels, and in the evening it hid away in the sauna, under a bench.

'What on earth's the matter with it?' the men wondered.

That same evening the men noticed a strong smell of smoke. As the lake grew smoother for the night, they could see, beyond the reeds of the farther shore, a blue cowl of smoke gathering.

'Somewhere there's a forest fire,' Vatanen said.

The next morning the smoke was enough to make their eyes smart. There was a wind on the lake, but the smoke thickened. It overlay everything like a dense sea-haze.

On the third morning of smoke Savolainen came running across the duckboard to the cabin.

'There's a huge fire at Vehmasjärvi. Vatanen, you'll have to go and join the fire-fighting gangs. Take Hannikainen's knapsack, and put some grub in. I'll spread the word round the villages. Let's be off straight away. Two thousand acres are up in smoke already.'

'Should I go too?' Hannikainen asked.

'No, you stay here with the hare. The over-fifty-fours don't have to go.'

Vatanen stuffed the knapsack with fish, lard, a pound of butter, and salt; then he left. Meanwhile, the hare was enticed into the cabin, so as not to follow Vatanen.

Vatanen was taken from Nilsiä to Rautavaara, where hundreds of men were gathering, some from the fire area, others on their way to it. Aircraft were continually droning overhead, lifting food from Rautavaara to the fire area. Tired, sooty men, back from the fire, had little to say about it; they crept into tents to sleep.

In a gap between the billeting tents, Rautavaara's elderly chemist had established a sort of first-aid station and, helped by his daughter, was binding fire-fighters' blistered legs and bathing them with boracic acid. A television crew was apparently interviewing the deputy town clerk of Rautavaara. The woman editor of the *Savo Daily Times* was taking photographs; Vatanen himself got his picture in the paper. Soup canteens were providing soup for all and sundry.

Trained orienteers were required. Vatanen said he could find his way in the wilds with a bucket on his head. A party of similar volunteers were herded into a heavy army helicopter.

Before the helicopter took off, the officer in charge explained what they had to do: 'I've photocopied the map of the area for each of you. Your copy gives you some idea how far the fire's got. Last night it came to a stop at the point marked on your map, but that's not where it is now. Right now it's travelling north-east through the tree-tops at a hellish speed. Tonight we'll be clearing a new firebreak seven miles farther up. During the night we're going to let over four thousand acres burn away. Half of it may, in fact, have gone already. We're dealing with the biggest fire in Finnish history, not counting Tuntsa perhaps. Now your task is this: you'll be let down at the point marked with a cross in the line of the fire's advance. You're to form a chain at hundred-yard intervals from each other and head north-east for at least six miles or so, shouting and making a hell of a row, to get the game to flee from the path of the fire. There are two houses as well. They'll have to be evacuated. Get the people down to the lake-shore, at this point here. And any other people, get them out of the fire area too. Also, according to our reports, there's livestock at large in these backwoods, on the run from Nilsiä – horses, and about fifty cows.

They've got to be driven down to the lake, to this point on the map, too.'

They helicoptered over the fire area. The glowing heat down below seemed to be reaching right up to the chopper. The air was cloaked in a thick pall of smoke, the earth scarcely visible. The helicopter was buffeted about in the heat turbulence, and it seemed as if the long blades of the main rotor might be going to crack and drop the chopper into the roaring furnace below.

The helicopter passed beyond the fire area and began descending like a large dragonfly. Its rotors chuntered; blue smoke jetted from the tail into the sweltering air. The lower the warplane got, the more the tree-tops swished. Finally the pine-cones on the ground flew helter-skelter in the hot down-draught; the helicopter touched down, and the roar of the rotors diminished.

The men leaped out and scurried out of range of the blades, bent double by the down-draught. The door banged shut, the rotors roared, and the chopper disappeared into the smoky air. The men were left rubbing their watering eyes in the forest.

Vatanen occupied a centre place in the chain. The men dispersed into the forest, their shouts echoing out of the smoky trees. Life does shake you up a bit, Vatanen was thinking: only a month ago he'd been sitting fed up to the back teeth in a corner tavern with a mug of warmish beer in his hand; and now here he was, in a hot wilderness, surrounded by smoke, carting round a knapsack of wet fish, and feeling the sweat running from his groin.

'Better a thousand times here, than in Helsinki.' He grinned, his eyes brimming with water.

The terrain descended into a damp depression. A large brown hare was zigzagging about, not knowing which way to go. Vatanen chased it the opposite way to the fire, and the creature vanished. In a dense clump of birches beyond the depression a cow was bellowing frantically. It was so panicked by all it had gone through, its bowels were loose: its flanks were spattered with cow-dung right up to the ridge of its back, and its tail was a smelly black whip. The cow stared at Vatanen with moist, fear-distended eyes, squeezing a stupid mooing from its swollen, panting throat. He grabbed it by the horns, screwed its head round with all his might, pointing it north-east, and kicked its backside. The poor creature finally got the point and disappeared the way it was supposed to go, with filth pouring from its rear and its bell clanking like a monastery fire-alarm. Vatanen wiped his watering eyes.

The forest was swarming with various animals: there were squirrels and hares; land fowl clacked into flight and splayed to earth again; he chased capercaillies like farmyard fowl to get them to understand which way to go. He came to a brook, a little river of clear water about four yards wide. Smoke hovered over the lush banks and the water: it had a fairy-tale beauty.

Vatanen took off his sweaty clothes and slipped naked into the cool water, rinsing his bloodshot eyes, rinsing fresh water in his mouth. After his trudge through the smoke a quiet dip in a brook was paradise. He swam slowly upstream, following the brook's interesting meandering. The water flowed slowly against him, and he felt blissful.

Suddenly he saw something by the thick grass on the river-bank: a man's hand – a hairy, sunburnt hand. It stretched out of the grass and rested in the water up to the elbow.

Vatanen was shocked: it looked as if the hand belonged to a corpse. He swam up to it and took hold of it. It was not unattached: it belonged to a large man lying back in the river-bank bushes with his mouth open. Vatanen got out of the water and bent down over the prone figure. He felt the pulse: it was beating normally. He put his face close to the man's mouth to see if he was breathing, and a foul reek of alcohol met him. Vatanen shook the man, who slowly began to come to. He turned on to his back and stared at Vatanen a moment as if trying to recognize him; then he offered his hand.

'Salosensaari. Who are you?'

'Vatanen.'

After they'd shaken hands, Vatanen helped the other man to his feet.

'Listen: you see the man who's been dealt the world's rottenest hand.'

He went on to explain. For his vacation, he'd decided to spend a couple of weeks fishing and also brewing a little moonshine in a quiet spot where he could be absolutely sure not to be disturbed. So he'd slipped off into the wilds with all his tackle and set up his modest still. Then, just as the first ten litres are cooked, what happens? A forest fire that incinerates his still. So he has to leg it full-tilt with the fire after him and a ten litre vat of hooch on his back. And now here he is: his knapsack and victuals are up in flames, everything's kaput, fishing tackle, the lot. All that's left is this first batch of the stuff.

'So here I am, parked here by the river. Second day, drinking, this is. Still quite a few litres left, but talk about rotten luck!'

Vatanen got a little camp-fire going on the river-bank and cooked some fish. Salosensaari went for a dip meanwhile, and then they both tucked in. After the meal Salosensaari offered some of his moonshine.

And why not? Vatanen accepted and swallowed some. Blessed stuff! It warmed the stomach. Vatanen took another nip.

'I'll tell you what, Salosensaari, you're a dab hand at making hooch.'

All afternoon the two went on boozing. From time to time they cooked fish or went for a swim. The more they drank, the less interest they felt in the whole forest-fire situation.

As evening approached, they were both so drunk it was with the greatest effort that they crawled out of the brook, which they were flopping into every now and then to refresh themselves. The brook was deep enough to reach their necks in places.

'Must watch out a bit. Don't want to drown by accident,' Salosensaari kept repeating.

In the night the fire reached the brook.

It was a fairyland. Blazing trees illuminated the night on both sides of the brook – huge red fluttering flowers. The heat was so scorching that while the fire lasted they had to stand in the brook: only their heads baked in the blazing glow. They had the vat of moonshine with them in the brook and tasted it liberally, watching with keen interest the destructive show of this wild natural super-star. The forest crashed, the fire thundered in the trees, hissing embers flew into the brook, the men's faces shone red upon the water, they laughed and tippled.

In the early hours the fire had passed by; the men emerged from the brook exhausted and dropped off to instant sleep on the charred river-bank.

They didn't wake till noon. Then they went their own ways, first shaking hands in farewell. Salonsensaari took the shortest route to Rautavaara, and Vatanen headed for the point by the lake where the evacuees were to congregate. The ashy road melted the rubber designs on the bottoms of his boots.

The fire had been brought to a halt a few miles away. Vatanen

crossed the firebreak and entered green forest. Soon he was at the
lake, where both people and animals were congregating. As for
the people, probably their houses had been burned down. The children were rollicking on the lake-shore; the cattle were bellowing
with fright in a meadow; the fire-fighters lay on the lake-shore
like sooty logs.

Vatanen handed over the rest of the fish in his knapsack to the
women, who began to make fish soup out of them in a cauldron
suspended over a camp-fire. Just as Vatanen was dropping off to
sleep, a bulldozer came rumbling to the shore. It emerged from
the fire area, crushing trees in its path; huge red pines were going
down under its digger, like willow-herb under a drunkard's boots.
It was pulling a large steel sleigh of men sitting with mechanical
saws and knapsacks at their feet.

The bulldozer thundered into the middle of the scene. Children
woke up crying, the cows in the meadow panicked, heaved to their
feet and started bellowing. The women yelled at the driver, berat-
ing him: coming and shaking everybody up like that, killing the
peace on the shore!

The driver couldn't hear what the women were shouting. He
switched off the engine and looked at them in bewilderment: it
was probably difficult to make out human voices after the din of
the bulldozer.

'Have you gone daft?' the women railed. 'Racketing in on everybody and everything like that? Couldn't you see you'd wake the
kids and scare the cows milkless?'

The driver wiped a sooty hand over his black face and said with
slow deliberation: 'Shut your faces, hags.'

'Don't you hag us, you nerd!' the women howled in fury.

The driver climbed down and walked over to the women. 'I've
been driving this bloody machine three days and three nights non-
stop without sleep. So shut your gobs.'

It showed. He looked dead-beat. Sweat had run great sooty streaks
down his cheeks: his weary face looked like smudged ink. He went
to the lake and rinsed his sooty face, cupping some water into his
mouth with his hands; gargling loudly, he spat the water back into
the lake. He returned with his face still wet, not willing to dry it
on his sooty sleeves. The cauldron of fish soup was bubbling on
the fire. He went to take a look at it, pulled a mess-tin out of his
knapsack and began ladling some soup for himself.

'Stop that!' the women shrieked. 'Who do you think you are? That's our fish soup!'

The man had managed to scoop a single ladle of savoury-smelling soup into his mess-tine. He took no more: he hurled the tin and soup back into the cauldron with a splash; the ladle he flung into the forest, too far to be heard dropping. He walked slowly over to his bulldozer, leaped athletically into the driving seat, started the huge machine up and pressed his heavy boot hard down on the accelerator. The engine roared, sparks showered up from the exhaust-pipe, and the machine clattered off, its broad tracks ripping up the smoothly trodden evening shoreline.

He aimed his machine straight at the fire and the steaming cauldron of fish soup. Nearing the fire, he lowered the digger; it scraped the ground, peeling off a three-foot-thick layer of earth, knocked the fire and the cauldron flying and ground them into the soil. Steam boiled up from the fish soup before both soup and cooking-gear disappeared under the turned soil. Nothing was left but a three-foot deep channel pointing to the lake. Three kinds of smell hovered in the air: fresh soil, burnt diesel, and the fading odour of fish soup.

The driver didn't stop after wiping out the fire: he accelerated the bulldozer to full speed. The machine broke through the bank by the lake; the ground gave way, the caterpillars clattered, the bushes swayed as the apparatus laboured through the bank and straight into the lake; the calm surface of the water was shattered. The digger pushed a large foaming wave into the heart of the lake. It was as if a steel hippopotamus had angrily taken to the water.

The lake bottom had a gradual slope: first the digger was immersed, then the caterpillars; as the water foamed into the tracks, the clatter changed to a squelching. The machine was butting a wave in front of it, which swilled farther and farther out. Shortly, water rose up to the red-hot engine: there were rumblings and bubblings as the lake-water boiled on the engine-sides. A thick cloud of steam plumed upwards, as if the machine had suddenly burst into flames.

But the driver forced his vehicle ever deeper: the water rose to the engine-top, the winch went under, and soon a wave was swilling over the bonnet. The machine went even deeper, the water swirled round the driver's buttocks, and simultaneously the engine slurped water inside. It coughed to a banging halt. The bulldozer was marooned a hundred yards from the shore.

The people on the shore watched in horror. The driver now turned on his seat, slowly got to his feet with his trousers dripping, and then sat on the floor of the cab. He turned shorewards and after a pause shouted in a voice that carried: 'Shut your gobs yet, have you?'

The women were whispering to each other: 'Lack of sleep it is. Driven him round the bend.'

The fire-fighters let rip: 'Blast you! You've ruined the soup!'

The man replied calmly: 'Did get spilt, I suppose.'

'Swim back now!' they shouted at him.

Nevertheless, he didn't attempt it. Instead, he climbed on to the steel bonnet, the only part still above water. He leaned against the exhaust-pipe, took his boots off and poured water into the lake.

Someone who knew told the others he couldn't swim.

There was no boat. They'd have to build a raft to get him off. The men with mechanical saws cursed: they were dead-beat from their nights without sleep at the firebreak; now they were supposed to start making a raft to rescue a lunatic bulldozer-driver sitting on his bonnet in the middle of a lake.

'Come on! What about a raft!' came a shout from the lake.

'Quit yelling. We will if we feel like it.'

The men conferred. One said that morning would be time enough. Perching out there for the night'd teach him a lesson.

They decided to make coffee before beginning work. When the driver saw no one was making a start, he went berserk: threats howled across the calm water. Finally, he yelled: 'You wait. The minute I'm back, I'll lay one on the lot of you.'

'Stone bonkers,' they decided.

He got more and more beside himself, hammering the metal bonnet with his fists. The banging carried across the lake to the far shore and sent the water-birds flocking into the air and sliding into the reeds.

All the same, the sawyers gradually put together a sort of raft: they bound logs together with rope, hewed a pole, but then retired on to the lakeside bank to think about sleep. No one was in a mood to set out and rescue a raving driver.

He was still howling from the bonnet of his bulldozer: 'You wait! First one I get hold of, I'll flatten him out in the bog!'

They pondered what to do. Poling out, on a scratch raft, to fetch a rather hefty near-homicidal maniac who'd gone several days without sleep, had no appeal for anyone. They'd fetch him off his machine in the morning, they decided: by then he might have calmed down a bit.

All night long the driver stormed on the lake. He yelled and yelled, though no one answered, till his voice became a croak. He kicked the bulldozer's headlights to smithereens. He twisted the exhaust-pipe off and threw the heavy metal object at the shore, which fortunately it didn't reach. Not till the small hours did he begin to tire; as dawn approached he snatched a couple of hours sleep belly-down on the bonnet.

At time for morning coffee, people began stirring, and the sounds woke the man on the steel bonnet. He began roaring again, slipped off his machine and flopped into the water.

That did bring things to life. The man was splashing about by his machine, yelling in terror. They slid the raft into the water. Vatanen and a sawyer started frantically poling it towards the bulldozer. The driver was making vain clutchings to climb on to his engine, but his hands slipped on the wet metal, and each time he fell back he went under and got more water in his lungs. His struggles became feebler and feebler, and finally he went completely under, floating face-down, only his spine poking up through his wet shirt.

Vatanen had managed to pole the raft to the precise spot; the two men hauled the driver aboard and turned his limp body on its side. Vatanen lifted the man's waist, letting water and mud flow from his mouth. The sawyer started poling back towards the shore; Vatanen knelt down and started administering mouth-to-mouth resuscitation, simultaneously pressing on the man's chest.

The driver was lifted ashore, where Vatanen continued his artificial respiration.

Perhaps five minutes elapsed before the drowned man showed any signs of revival. Then his body stiffened, his hands began to tremble, and finally Vatanen heard the driver's teeth grating together. He was thankful his own tongue hadn't been caught between the other's teeth.

As soon as the driver came to, he grabbed Vatanen and pitched into him: for a moment the rescuer had to tussle with him unaided before the others realized they ought to come and give a hand. With the help of several men, the driver was finally forced to give in and roped to a stump sticking up on the shore. There they left him, sitting with his back to the stump.

'A hard case,' they said.

'Let me go! I'll yank this stump up with me!' he threatened, but nevertheless he didn't try to carry out his threat. Instead he fell into a subdued muttering: 'Bloody lot! Leave a man out there, who can't swim, all night long, in the middle of a lake. I'll have the bloody police on them.'

Several soldiers came to fetch him, and he was taken off into the forest on a stretcher, on to which he had to be strapped.

A terrible wailing came from the forest, only dying away much later, when the stretcher was a mile or two off.

9 In the Marsh

A new morning dawned. Vatanen was woken by the racket of motor vehicles: three Land Rovers had ploughed their way through the forest and got to the lake. The men in them included the two superintendents, Hannikainen and Savolainen. Hannikainen had a knapsack on his back: a hare's head peeped from under the flap.

Vatanen rushed over to them, grabbed the knapsack off Hannikainen's back, undid the cord and welcomed the hare into his arms. What a happy reunion!

The hare sniffed Vatanen excitedly. When he put it on the ground, it ran happily round his legs like a little dog.

Savolainen took charge on the shore; his orders were to superintend evacuation of personnel and animals.

Hannikainen was there out of curiosity; time had probably been dragging a little, with his friends away fire-fighting.

'I got such a haul of pike, I had to go round the villages selling it off. I took the hare along. I laid off my research for a bit,' he added. Taking Vatanen on one side, he whispered: 'I made a few more calculations back there, though. They show that President Kekkonen – the new one, that is – will still be there in 1995. By my reckoning, "The New Kekkonen" will then be only about seventy-five, whereas the old one would have been ninety. I fear it'll cause a lot of unfortunate speculation abroad. They won't know what's going on really.' He added: 'Theoretically it's perfectly possible for Kekkonen to be still governing the country after the year 2000. By then he'll be eighty-five. In my opinion, though, he'll not dare offer himself as president in the next millennium.'

Tents were erected on the bank by the lake; soup canteens were heated up; blankets were distributed. A large winch was unloaded from the back of a Land Rover and set up onshore. Its purpose was to haul the bulldozer out of the lake.

Since he'd not been allotted any other task, Vatanen went into the meadow to help the women with the milking. One young woman, Irja, had already milked three plastic pailfuls of milk, and Vatanen helped her carry them over to a spring of water, for cooling. Soon the hare came hopping over as well. Irja fell for the hare at once.

'Oh, what a darling!'

'Would you like to take it to bed with you?'

Irja certainly would.

'You can, if you like. Provided you take me as well. Are you on?'

In the evening the three of them, Vatanen, Irja Lankinen and the hare, retired to a barn in the meadow for the night. Vatanen had taken some blankets there. Irja brought some soup from the tents. She made up beds by the back wall of the barn, Vatanen closed the barn door, the sun went down, and then there was a voice inside the barn: 'Stop it. It's looking.'

The barn door flew open, and the hare flew out. Vatanen had chucked it into the meadow. The door closed; the hare sat there in the dusk, embarrassed. Half an hour later, Vatanen came to the door and apologized for throwing it out. The hare slipped in, the door closed again, and there was quiet everywhere. Even the curlews were quiet on the lake.

In the morning Savolainen asked Vatanen if he'd mind accompanying Irja about eight miles through the forest to the Sonkajärvi road. She was herding some cows there to be loaded into cattle-trucks and driven to cowsheds in Sonkajärvi. Vatanen was delighted: nothing could be better than cowherding with Irja. In some elation, he said goodbye to Savolainen and Hannikainen.

Hannikainen said: 'If you ever come Nilsiä way, look me up. I'll definitely have my research complete by then.'

It was a gorgeous day. They sang as they went along. The sun shone, there was no hurry. From time to time, they let the cows browse peacefully along the ditches, and at midday the beasts lay down for an hour or two, ruminating. Meanwhile the cowherds went for a swim. Irja looked marvellous, sinking into the cool forest mere with her sumptuous breasts.

In the afternoon a large brown cow began complaining. It moaned quietly, closing its moist eyes, and showing unwilling to keep up with the other cows. Nor would it eat with the others; it just drank water. It strayed from the herd, mooing querulously, and walked between two trees, leaning a flank against one, and turning to look at Irja.

'That one's going to calve soon,' Irja said anxiously.

To Vatanen the cow didn't look any more round-bellied than the others, but no doubt Irja knew what she was talking about.

'If we're not at the road soon, she'll have it here in the forest,' Irja said.

'What if I go ahead to Sonkajärvi,' Vatanen said, 'and bring a vet?'

'Rubbish! It can throw it here. It's healthy enough, that cow. And as for you, you're certainly up to carrying a calf.'

After a while the cow began to paw the ground and arch its back, clearly in pain. It let out urgent intermittent lowings, sounds you'd never expect from a cow. Irja spoke consolingly to it; the beast responded by mooing more quietly. Finally it went to lie down.

After an hour Irja said: 'It's on its way. Come and help me pull it out.'

The calf came out slowly, the cow groaning agonizedly; they had to pull hard. Then the calf dropped to the ground – the cow had heaved to its feet. The calf was slimy with mucus, and the cow, completely at peace already, began licking it.

Vatanen dug a pit a hundred yards away and buried the after-birth. He came back to Irja and the calf, which was trying to struggle to its feet but continually flopping back, still too weak. It did know how to suck on a teat: it knelt down under the cow and gorged itself.

Obviously a new-born calf like that couldn't totter through the forest to the road. Should it be killed? Definitely not. Irja and Vatanen settled for Irja to go on ahead with the cows, and Vatanen would carry the calf on his shoulders, bringing up the rear with the mother cow.

He pulled a blanket out of his knapsack, tied rope to the corners and constructed a sort of hammock that he could carry on his back. As he squeezed the calf into the blanket-bag, it lowed with fear, but to no avail. It was still quite incapable of managing on its own legs. The cow looked on calmly as the calf was tucked into the blanket.

Vatanen heaved the calf on to his back; its hoofs tapped the back of his neck rhythmically as he plodded along. The hare was somewhat nonplussed. It loped nervously about at Vatanen's feet but then settled down to the slow advance. Calf on back, Vatanen led the way forward through the forest. The pensive cow ambled quietly behind him, occasionally licking her calf's head; and the hare undulated along at the rear.

It surprised Vatanen that the calf didn't get a stomach upset, swinging in its hammock to the rhythm of his tread. But it had been swinging many months like that in its mother's belly. What a trip! Burdened by his calf, Vatanen was in a sweat. Gnats had come out too: they were flying into his nostrils and, with both his hands gripping the ropes, and the knapsack dangling on his belly, he couldn't reach up to flick them away.

'Loving animals can be a heavy load,' he muttered to himself as a sprig of spruce lashed his face in a thicket.

But Vatanen's load was not yet full.

He took a short cut through a bog. 'I'm not going to circle round that,' he decided. 'It'd put half a mile on, at the very least.' He tested the bog: it seemed to hold him up. The cow hesitated: should it follow? But when Vatanen turned and ordered it to follow, it summoned up courage. Its hoofs did sink a bit, but Vatanen calculated that, in a dry summer like this, a sphagnum-moss bog would support a single cow; and besides, the cattle on these outlying farms were able to cope with bogs.

But towards the centre, the bog turned squashier. The swamp began to give under the cow: it needed to break into a canter if it wasn't going to sink in the ooze. There was no headway to be made in the mire; so they had to take a detour along some ridges of sphagnum moss. In the slushier spots, Vatanen himself had to break into a half-trot, and half-way across the swamp his boots stuck in the mud. He gave his leg a furious yank, but his boot remained stuck, and then the other stuck too. With an awkward effort he managed to jump barefoot on to a dry spot.

From behind came a lowing. He swung round anxiously to look. The cumbersome cow had been athletically following his footsteps, but now it could no longer keep up. It had sunk to its belly in the bog: it lay there motionless, mooing for help.

Vatanen dropped the calf on a sphagnum hummock and ran to the cow's help. He tried hauling it by the horns on to a drier patch, but no man is strong enough to heave a cow out of a swamp.

He had to move fast. Whipping an axe out of his knapsack, he ran fifty yards to some little dead trees that were sticking up out of the marsh. Chopping several down, he stripped the sharp twigs off them and ran back to the cow, which had sunk a little deeper still.

He thrust the rods he'd made under the cow's belly. The beast seemed to understand that the intention was good: it didn't thrash about, even though thin trunks shoved under its belly may well have been hurtful. The sinking stopped. Vatanen tried to prise the beast higher, but with very little success. The cow was spattered with black mud. The hare loped about in astonishment.

'Why don't *you* do something?' Vatanen snarled, as he prised and heaved at the cow. But the hare didn't help, hare-brained and helpless as it was.

Vatanen broke off to go and calm the calf, which was on a hummock. He untied the blanket ropes, fastened them end to end, and then went back to fasten the rope round the cow's shoulders. The cow's dewlap was deep in mud, and Vatanen was soon black with mud from head to foot.

The rope just reached as far as the stump of an old marsh redwood five yards away. Vatanen tied it securely to the stump.

'If you sink now, then that stump'll sink with you,' he told the cow.

Anchored to the stump, the cow listened calmly to his words: it made no lowing when it saw him busying himself nearby.

Vatanen made a tourniquet by separating the strands of the rope and pushing a stick into the gap. Then he began to turn. Soon the rope tightened. The cow's legs began rising slowly out of the mud. The beast did its best to co-operate. From time to time Vatanen relaxed the tourniquet and went to prise up the cow's backside, being careful not to injure the udder. The cow was gradually moving towards the stump.

Turn and turn about, Vatanen reeled the cow stumpwards, went back to prise the beast up, calmed it.

During all this labour, time was flashing by so quickly it was evening before Vatanen noticed. He was weary, but he couldn't leave the cow lying in the marsh all night.

'No joke, this cowherding!'

By midnight Vatanen had got the cow into a good enough position for it to struggle out by itself. The beast summoned its last strength for a spurt from the mud and, finding solid ground under it, lay down immediately. Vatanen led the tottering calf to its dam and dropped off to sleep on the hummock himself. It turned cold in the early hours, and he moved over to sleep against the cow's flank. It was as warm as a chimney-corner.

The morning sun rose on a mucky retinue: a black mud-bespattered cow; a black, mud-bespattered man; a black, mud-bespattered calf; and a black, mud-bespattered hare. They woke. The cow shat, the calf sucked milk, Vatanen smoked a cigarette. Then he set off, carrying the calf to the far edge of the marsh. The cow followed more gingerly than before, and when it got to the other side, it turned to stare at the bog and bellow at it angrily.

At the next pool in the forest Vatanen washed the cow down, then the calf, and rinsed his own clothes. He had no boots: they were back there in the mud. Last of all, he washed the hare. It was outraged for quite a while.

When Vatanen and his train of animals reached the Sonkajärvi road, an empty cattle-truck awaited him, and some tired men who had been vainly searching for him all night long. The other cattle had been driven away the previous evening, along with a worried Irja. Vatanen too was driven to Sonkajärvi in the cattle-truck, and soon he was standing in the village high street, wearing smutty, mud-bespattered clothes, clutching a hare in his arms, and barefoot.

10 In the Church

Vatanen spent the night in a boarding-house. He had a poor night in a good bed, for he was now accustomed to life in the open air. In the morning he went shopping for new boots, a pullover, underclothes, trousers, everything. He threw his dirty old clothes in a rubbish bin.

It was a hot, sunny morning, and Saturday as well. He took a stroll round the village streets and, in his search for a good spot for the hare to browse, he came across the cemetery.

The herbaceous arrangements on the little hillocks were very much to the hare's taste. It particularly relished the rye-grass on the recent spring graves.

The church door was unlocked. Vatanen called the hare away from the grave-plots and took it inside. What a wonderful coolness and peace! Though Vatanen had long since given up church, it didn't stop him relishing the silence of the huge space.

The hare hopped along the central aisle to the chancel, dropped a few innocent pills in front of the altar, and then began studying the church more systematically. Vatanen sat down in a pew, observing the altar painting and the architecture of the nave. There were places for about six hundred people there, he estimated. The nave was partially two-level: both side-walls were lined full-length with galleries that joined under the organ-loft at the back. Wooden staircases led to the galleries from either side of the altar. A looming light from the high, narrow windows evoked a dreamy, peaceful ambience.

He gathered up the hare-droppings from the altar and slipped them in his pocket. He picked his way down a side-aisle to a pew tucked away at the back, removed his shiny new boots, stretched out on the bench, settled the knapsack under his head and prepared for a doze. This was a much more agreeable place for sleeping than the boarding-house. The eye could travel into the lofty Christian spaces of the ceiling, and the still, pitch-pine columns adorned with verses were a fine contrast to the grubby designs on the peeling boarding-house wallpaper. The hare was silently pottering about by the sacristy door behind the altar. Let it, Vatanen thought, and dozed off.

While he was sleeping, an elderly man came into the church: the pastor, here to do a few ecclesiastical chores. He was wearing his ministerial garb, a black cassock with the white tabs of his clerical bands at the neck. He walked briskly past the altar to the sacristy without noticing the hare near the door. It stared in astonishment at this apparition of a black-cassocked man.

Presently the pastor came out of the sacristy hugging a collection of long candles and a pile of paper, probably the scrumpled-up packing paper. He went up the steps to the altar, removed the guttered candles from their candlesticks and replaced them with new ones. He took the candle-ends back into the sacristy and simultaneously dispensed with the ball of paper.

Returning, he lit the candles and retreated into the central aisle to appreciate the result. He tapped his pocket through the cassock, rattling a box of matches. He produced a cigarette and lit up, blowing the smoke away from the altar with each puff. When the cigarette burned down he stubbed it on a stone window-sill, blew the ash on to the floor, put the stump in his matchbox and thrust the box in his pocket. Finally he rubbed his hands on the hem of his cassock, as if to wipe away his sin of smoking.

He again went into the sacristy. When he came back, he was holding several sheets of paper, probably sermons.

Only now did he perceive the hare, which had lolloped its way up to the altar. It had profanely left a few droppings by the sacred place, and now it was sniffing the flower arrangements on the altar steps.

The pastor was shocked into letting the sheets of paper slip from his hands and float down to the floor.

'Lord help us!'

The hare hopped down the altar steps and vanished into a side-aisle.

Vatanen woke. He rose from his sleeping position and saw the hare flashing to the back of the church and the shocked pastor wiping sweat from his forehead.

He sank back behind the pew to follow what happened unobserved.

The elderly pastor recovered rather fast. He cautiously crept into the side-aisle and saw the hare sitting up on its hind legs at the other end: a charming creature in a graceful pose.

'Puss-puss-puss-puss-puss!' he coaxed, but the hare didn't trust the invitation: the rector was in such a stew the hare scented danger.

The pastor made a faster rush than seemed possible for such an elderly man and tried to trap the hare under his cassock. No luck: the hare was faster.

'It's very sharp, but I've got to get it.'

The hare circled round the other side of the church to the altar. The pastor stole along the central aisle, slightly out of breath, approaching the altar too. When he reached the critical distance, the hare dashed up the stairway to the gallery. The pastor didn't follow at once. He collected his papers off the floor, arranged them on the altar rail and then noticed the droppings by the altar.

In dismay, he picked the droppings up and threw them into the pulpit one by one, not missing with a single throw. He rested a moment and then clambered up the steps to the gallery. The heavy beams creaked under his feet as he trod his way to the back. Suddenly he broke into a thundering rush: he'd caught sight of the hare, but the hare was off again. The rector shouted: 'Don't worry, I'll get you in the end. You may be a wild animal but... puss-puss-puss!'

The frightened hare ran round the opposite gallery, dashed down the stairway and hid in the sacristy door behind the altar. The old clergyman ran the same route and came clomping down the stairs. Completely puffed, he didn't see the hare crouching in the sacristy doorway.

He glanced at his watch, went to the church door, banged it to, and locked it. This done, he prowled the central aisle like a hunter stalking. Then he saw the hare.

'Now you're trapped, you little devil!' he muttered as he passed Vatanen. Playing cool, he skirted the altar a yard or two from the hare, which thought it wasn't seen. Then the pastor made a tremendous leap at the sacristy door: arms wide, he trapped the hare underneath him. The hare gave a pitiable, piercing whimper like a baby, then managed to wriggle free from the old man's embrace and tore blindly down the centre aisle towards the church door.

'Oh my God!'

The clergyman was lying on his belly in the sacristy door, a tuft of hare-fur in his hand.

Before Vatanen could get to him, the clergyman was on his feet and out of the church; through a window Vatanen saw him hop on to a bicycle and ride frantically off towards the parsonage. Soon he was pedalling fiercely back up the hill to the church. Vatanen scarcely had time to hide in a pew before the pastor had swept through the door.

He hastened to the central aisle. There he stopped and pulled a Mauser pistol out of his cassock. He checked the magazine, released the safety-catch. His eyes glinted in the dimness of the church, searching for the hare.

It was crouching near the altar. Catching sight of it, the pastor raised his pistol and fired. The hare leaped off in terror, while a smell of cordite floated down the central aisle. The pastor pounded round the flank; two successive reports crashed out. The bullets whistled through the ecclesiastical air, while Vatanen ducked behind his pew like a patron in a Wild West saloon.

The pastor did two circuits of the church, firing after the hare on both loops. Running up the central aisle again, he pulled up in shock to stare at the altar painting: a Mauser bullet had ripped through the canvas. It was a picture of the Redeemer on the Cross, and the bullet had pierced Christ's kneecap.

The Mauser went off yet again – this time pointing downwards and obviously by mistake. The pastor groaned and lifted his right leg. The smoking weapon slipped from his hand; he began to weep. Vatanen ran up to him and picked the gun off the floor.

The bullet had pierced the middle of the pastor's black patent-leather shoe. Black blood was dripping from the sole. There was a hole in the church floor at the point where the pastor's foot had just been.

'I'm the Reverend Laamanen,' he whimpered, standing on one foot and offering his hand to Vatanen. Vatanen shook him by the hand, being careful not to tip him over.

'Vatanen.'

Laamanen hopped along on one leg to the sacristy. At each hop blood dripped out of his shoe on to the floor. Vatanen wiped it up with his handkerchief; the blood came away easily, being still wet.

'I got carried away, seeing that hare. I've had this gun since 1917. I was in the infantry, you see, a lieutenant. What got hold of me? And a stray bullet's pierced that painting! How can God ever forgive me, shooting his only Son in the knee, here in his own house!'

He wept. Vatanen was feeling pretty bad about it himself. He said he'd go to the parsonage and ring an ambulance.

'No, no! Be a good fellow and get this smell of cordite out. The town clerk's daughter'll be here any minute to get married. Let's just put a bandage on. I've got to marry this couple first. And would you please be kind enough too to gather up any cartridge cases you see lying around in the aisles. Kick them into a corner.'

Vatanen went round opening the church windows. The smell slowly vanished from the church on to the hill. He found several empty cartridge cases and stuffed them in his pocket. In the sacristy he tore a small altar cloth into strips and put a temporary bandage on Laamanen's foot. Laamanen was wearing insoles in his shoes. Vatanen changed them round, putting the blood-soaked one with its bullet-hole in the good shoe, and the undamaged insole in the damaged shoe: that way the shoes were almost restored. At any rate, for the time being, the insole would stop blood seeping from the bandage on to the floor.

Voices were already audible from the nave. The marital couple were arriving with their relatives. The clergyman hobbled to the sacristy door. Vatanen opened it and guided him altarwards. Once in the chancel Laamanen walked steadily, as if there were nothing wrong with his foot.

Vatanen settled down for the wedding at the back of the church; he found the hare pottering about there as well. It hopped into Vatanen's lap and remained there during the service.

Laamanen married the couple with practised skill. After the ceremony he delivered a short address. His eyes were moist, and several of the women, interpreting the moistness in their own way, began to sob. There was a moving atmosphere of utmost devotion. The men cleared their throats behind their hands as discreetly as possible.

'It was God himself who created the institution of marriage, and our newly-married friends here, like others, should hold fast to that. You see, what God, in his great mercy, has ordained is sacred. Too sacred to be profaned. Yet marriage is full of lurking dangers, and one of these terrible lurking dangers is jealousy. Jealousy rages around like a hungry lion, bringing an unhappy mind. Today you two, my dear friends, feel a deep sense of belonging to each other, and mutual love. Yet a time may well come, and a day, when some other person may seem still more dear. If that happens, I want you to remember these words from the Bible: "What then? Notwithstanding, in every way, whether in pretence, or in truth, Christ is preached; and I therein do rejoice." I quote from the Epistle of Paul the Apostle to the Philippians, Chapter I, verse 18, and these devout words I pass on to you as guardians of your marriage. In a time of need, take them out, read them! Then the drizzle of delusory love will pass over, and your soul will find its peace. I hope you'll both be very happy.'

Laamanen gave the married couple a white-bound Bible and shook their hands. He stood firm on both feet till the congregation had filtered out and the door finally closed. Then he carefully raised his foot. The church floor was stamped with a large blood-stained footprint.

Vatanen hurried to the parsonage to ring Kuopio for a taxi. While he waited, the Reverend Laamanen lay on a pew, quietly sobbing.

'What can that marriage come to, since I, figuratively speaking, performed it in blood-stained clothes. My dear Vatanen, swear by Almighty God you'll never relate what happened here in this church today.'

Vatanen gave his word. Then the taxi came. Before hobbling into it, Laamanen knelt before the altar painting, clasped his hands and prayed: 'Lord Jesus, only-begotten Son of God, forgive me for what I have done to thee today. But in the name of our Almighty Father, what happened was an accident!'

Vatanen told the taximan to drive quickly to the outpatients department of Kuopio General Hospital. Laamanen eased himself into the taxi, and soon it had vanished up the dusty road.

Vatanen stretched out full length on a pew, and the hare too fell asleep on the floor. It was tired. The silence, now complete again in the nave, lulled them both into a profound slumber.

11 Grandad

Towards the end of July Vatanen took a forestry job: it meant billhooking and chopping excessive undergrowth from the afforestation on the sandy ridges round Kuhmo and living in a tent with a more-and-more faithful, almost fully-grown hare.

He was now seventy or eighty miles still farther north, about half-way up the map of Finland. He performed his heavy labour with no concern for time; he grew tougher and thought less and less about the flabby life he'd left three hundred miles or so south in the capital city. Here there were no boring political arguments with raw proselytes, and no randy women displaying themselves for picking and choosing. In the Kuhmo forest wilderness he could keep sex obsession out of his head.

Anyone could live this life, he reflected, provided they had the nous to give up the other way of life.

He'd been clearing undergrowth without stop for a couple of weeks and had finished his assignment: the privileged saplings had been given enough space to grow; it was time to be off to the township of Kuhmo and get paid.

Around midnight he arrived at a little village on the shore of Lake Lentua. His seven-mile trek had wearied him, and he'd have liked to put up at some house; but the village was asleep, and he didn't feel like waking anyone in the middle of the night. So he went into a windowless, timbered barn in the yard of a large farmhouse, threw his knapsack by the wall and settled down to sleep on the floor. It's very pleasant sleeping in black darkness: the mosquitoes don't bother you: people who live in the forest think such sleep is a luxury. The hare was restless, though. It kept sniffing the air round it; the barn had an odour of rotten fish. They've not put enough salt in the carp-tub, Vatanen decided, and dropped off, giving little thought to the sweetish smell.

At about six he woke and rose with stiff limbs, rubbing his eyes in the dark barn and thinking the farm people would soon be stirring: he'd be able to get some coffee. The hare was lying by the wall, behind his knapsack. It was very agitated, as if it hadn't slept the whole night.

He made his way into the middle of the barn and stumbled over something he hadn't noticed the night before. He felt it: his hand met a thick peg stuck into a plank. It was a bench for planing. This was a work-bench in the middle of the floor.

He circled round to the other side of the bench, feeling his way along the bench-top in the dark. His hand met some cloth. Taken by surprise, he started groping at the bench-top to see what was on it.

Someone seemed to be asleep there under a sheet. Astonishing! It must have been a very deep sleep for him not to wake when Vatanen opened the door in the night.

'Wake up, mate,' Vatanen said, but got no reply. The sleeper evidently hadn't heard: at any rate, he showed no sign of waking. Vatanen touched the sleeper a little more enquiringly: it was definitely a man sleeping on the bench-top, under a cloth, without a pillow. His arms were straight down his sides, his boots were off, he had a large nose. Gently, Vatanen began shaking the sleeper; he raised him into a sitting position and addressed him.

Then he decided to open the door: the light would wake him. Starting towards the door, he felt his pocket catch on the handle of the vice: the whole bench tilted, and the sleeper came rolling off. There was an audible thump as his head hit the ground. Vatanen wrenched the barn door open, and the light showed him that an old man was lying unconscious on the floor.

Vatanen flapped: 'He's banged his head!'

He went over to the man, felt round his heart in panic, but couldn't make out whether it was beating or not. Anyway, the man had clearly been concussed by his fall. In consternation, Vatanen carefully picked the unconscious man up and carried him out into the yard. There, in the bright morning light, he studied the man's face. Calm, furrowed features, eyes shut. An elderly man like that could easily die from a fall off a bench. Better move fast. The unconscious man lay across his chest like something on a tray. He ran into the middle of the yard, heading for the farmhouse, but, luckily, just then a young woman appeared on the doorsteps, carrying milk cans.

Vatanen gave a shout: 'There's been an accident!' There he stood in the middle of the yard with an unconscious old man in his arms, saying: 'I can explain this! But get someone who can do first aid!'

The milkmaid panicked in turn. The cans dropped from her plump hands, clattered down the steps and rolled across the yard to the well. She darted inside and Vatanen was left on the lawn, holding the man in his arms. The concussed man's condition seemed to have got even worse. A flood of compassion swept over Vatanen – he hadn't wanted to cause any harm!

People in underclothes were appearing on the doorsteps: the farmer, his wife, and the same young woman. But they were too shocked themselves to rush and help Vatanen resuscitate the man.

'You haven't a swing, have you?' Vatanen shouted. 'That gets them breathing again.'

But they were silent, no one made a move to help.

Finally the farmer said: 'It's our grandad. Take him back.'

Vatanen was nonplussed. 'Take him back' reverberated a moment in his thoughts. He looked at 'grandad' lying stiff in his arms. One eyelid had half opened. Vatanen looked into the eye.

Then he realized. He was holding a dead man: long dead. A gruesome feeling made him go weak: the burden fell from his arms on to the lawn. The farmer rushed down the steps and lifted the corpse on his back. The deceased man teetered a little, but the farmer strengthened his grip, took him back into the barn, laid him out on the bench and covered him up with the sheet. Then he closed the barn door and came back into the yard.

'You've desecrated our grandad!'

Vatanen scarcely heard, for he was vomiting behind the well.

Explanations followed.

Vatanen had spent the night with the head of the house, who had died the evening before. The house was in deep mourning, for he'd been a grand old man. Forgiveness for the misconception now followed, but when they spoke of the old grandad, the women wept. Vatanen too felt a lump in his throat. The hare sat at a distance like a partner in crime.

At ten o'clock a hearse drew up in the yard. Vatanen helped the farmer transfer the corpse to the vehicle. They closed the eye that had opened in Vatanen's arms, the driver presented a form, and the farmer signed it.

Vatanen was given a lift to Kuhmo in the hearse. Behind, the coffin looked very dignified under its black pall.

The undertaker chatted on and on about the hare and revealed that he himself had a tame magpie in Kajaani.

'It'd stolen a reflector, from the chief constable's wife, so I heard, right in the middle of the town. Anyway that's what it flew in the house with.... By the way, changing the subject, I knew this Heikkinen, the old chap. Communist he was, in his time, but he didn't get fat on that. Turn communist, and you'll never get rich.'

12 *Kurko*

As July turned to August Vatanen got as far as Rovaniemi, on the
Arctic Circle. The last logs had floated down past the town, and
there were fewer tourists than usual.

In the ground-floor room of Rovaniemi's Lapland Restaurant
Vatanen met an old lumberjack, a luckless drinker called Kurko.
In his youth, in the hard-bitten lumbercamps of those days, Kurko
had been known in Lapland as *metsien kuningas* – the king of the
forests'. This had been shortened to the nickname 'Kurko', Finnish
for an evil spirit.

Kurko was grumbling about his lot: there was no work for him
nowadays in the forests: too old, and a drunk besides. He ought to
be seeing about an old-age pension, but that'd hardly keep a free-
ranging maverick like himself going. Life was hard for an old tree-
feller.

Vatanen was pondering how he could help the old man.

He managed to get a small job with the Lapland branch of the
TVH, the Water and Forest Authority. His contract was to break
up three log-rafts on the River Ounasjoki, north of the village of
Meltaus.

Kurko was eager to come along as mate, and they took off up-
river for their job.

Once there, they winched the rafts ashore, They had rented a mechanical saw, and they began dismantling the cumbersome old rafts
with iron handspikes and other tools. The work went well in the
early autumn weather. They lived in a tent and did their cooking over
a camp-fire in front of the tent. Kurko grumbled about his thirst, but
otherwise he too was content enough with the demolition work.

People from the village wandered to the site from time to time. They boggled, in their slow northern way, at the hare. Vatanen asked the farmers not to let their dogs loose, and it was only rarely that the hare did come tearing in from the village with a dog at its heels. When that happened, the hare dashed into the camp, leaped into Vatanen's arms, or slipped into the tent, and the dogs had to trot disappointedly back to the village.

When two of the rafts had been dismantled and the timber stacked, Vatanen paid Kurko two weeks' wages. At once Kurko scarpered to Rovaniemi. He was away three days. When he came back, he was dead drunk and skint, in the manner to which he was accustomed. The binge went on for another night, and it might have taken a very nasty turn, for Kurko wanted to show what a good logger he was. He went dancing along the floating logs that girdled the river-bank, missed his footing, flopped in the river and was on the point of drowning, for he couldn't swim. Vatanen hauled the drunken old-timer out of the chilly river and carried him to their tent. In the morning Kurko woke up with a blinding hangover; he felt hard done by, opened his mouth to complain, and realized his false teeth had gone to feed the fish. Life can be dampening sometimes.

A day later Kurko was restored to animation. He couldn't eat anything but gruel, though, and naturally he felt the pangs of hunger. 'Teach me to swim,' he begged.

Vatanen inaugurated swimming lessons the very same evening. Strip naked, he told him; and when Kurko was starkers, Vatanen made him lie on his belly in the water, gripping on to the bank with his hands.

If it's difficult to teach an old dog to sit, as they say, then it's even more difficult to teach an old Lapland roué to swim. Poor old Kurko did his level best, but progress was slow. Evening after evening the routine went on. Vatanen was astounded at Kurko's dead-set persistence.

Finally a wonder occurred.

Kurko learned to swim dog-paddle. The water held him up! Roars of triumph echoed round the banks when he discovered his new prowess. He was so keen, he splashed about till late evening, sometimes swimming underwater for long spells, letting the current take him and then bobbing up, snorting, yards and yards downstream. His hardened old carcass stood the cold water well, and joy in his new-found life-style beamed from his wrinkly face.

'It's Sunday tomorrow, I'll go diving for those false teeth,' he decided. He was so besotted with swimming, he didn't even go for the Saturday-night sauna but went on messing about in the river.

Kurko could hold out for minutes under the water. It showed the next day as he went diving to the bottom of the Ounasjoki for his false teeth. A crowd of villagers gathered to watch him from the bank; some had come to see the hare. In general, the two demolitioners were thought rather weird, and no doubt with reason: one of them went around with a tame hare, and the other spent the whole day floundering about in the chilly river. A tourist bus pulled up at the spot, and about forty Germans came to gape at the spectacle. Someone took out an amateur camera and filmed Kurko. The guide explained to his compatriots that this was training for the coming Lapland logging competitions.

In the evening, Kurko told Vatanen he'd not found his false teeth but something much more valuable.

'Round about mid-stream, it's over thirty feet deep. I found something down there – a hundred tons at least of war gear. Twenty-odd big guns, at least one tank, some large boxes, loads of stuff. That's what all the diving was about. . . . Give us five hundred and I'll flog that junk.'

A remarkable find, and a remarkable man, this Kurko. Vatanen slipped his clothes off, picked his way over the floating logs to the river and dived down deep. The current was very strong, and it was difficult to get to the right spot.

Kurko had not been making it up. Vatanen banged his knee on a steel snag, examined the obstacle close up and concluded that an artillery piece was indeed lying on its side on the river-bed. Amazing that it hadn't been discovered earlier! But the top of the gun was covered with sunken, waterlogged lumber from decades of felling.

Vatanen gave Kurko his five hundred, and the old-stager left at dawn for Rovaniemi. Vatanen stayed behind and got on with breaking up the last raft alone.

Again Kurko was delayed in town: two days this time. Back again, he was drunk but happy. There was still some of the cash left; and there was booze: many a bottle of high-class brandy. Tipsily Kurko bragged: 'Take a look at King Dick. Tomorrow morning you'll see things rolling.'

This said, he was out like a light, and Vatanen had no idea what Kurko had set in motion.

In the morning three massive lorries marked HEAVY-DUTY HAULAGE rumbled into the camp. Kurko had evidently inaugurated a mega-operation.

Disregarding his hangover, Kurko set to work. He took charge, ordered Vatanen and the lorrymen to manoeuvre a large winch into position between two massive red pines on the shore. It was a heavy contraption with a hauling power of twenty tons. They anchored it to the massive pine-trunks with thick cables. A smaller winch, set up on the opposite shore, pulled the big winch's tow-cable into the river.

Kurko took a dive, leading the heavy end of the tow-cable down with him. He was out of sight for a long time. Then he emerged, snorting. He gave a shout: 'Haul away!'

The tow-cable tightened; the tops of the pines swayed, but the winch's anchorage held. The river-bank's girdle of floating logs sank under the pressure of the cable, which slowly wound itself round the hub of the winch. A minute later, a mighty rusty howitzer rose out of the water: a six-incher. German made. Kurko splashed to the shore in glee and took a swig of the brandy. 'To warm myself up,' he explained.

The rusty weapon was hauled on to a lorry and fastened down. Vatanen made a note of its weight, since the crane sported a hydraulic balance.

All day long Kurko swam from shore to midstream and tirelessly pursued his exhausting work. Eleven pieces of heavy artillery were hauled up, a score of anti-aircraft guns, one fifteen-ton tank, and many boxes of ammunition. The whole caboodle must have been dumped during the German retreat in the Lapland war, but it was amazing the cache had not been spotted before.

'And now drive it off to Kolari station. You'll find the railway trucks there waiting, booked in my name. Load this stuff on them, and here's the bills of freight.'

Kurko handed the lorrymen a bundle of papers.

'As soon as you've got the stuff in the trucks, get back for the rest, even if it's night. You'll have the money in a week, and you can have my signature now.'

Kurko signed for the haulage costs, and the great lorries rumbled off. Vatanen had been somewhat flabbergasted by the spectacle, and he was not the only one. The people from Meltaus had heard about Kurko's new role and were boggling at his business transactions.

The next day the last of the war material was hauled out of the river, and in the early afternoon the vehicles made their last trip from Meltaus to Kolari. Kurko said he'd sold the scrap metal direct to the steel works in Koverhar on the south coast; now all they had to do was wait till Friday, when the money would be wired to the bank in Rovaniemi. Ovako, the firm, would pay for the scrap metal only when it was on the factory rails.

A reporter from the *Lapland News* turned up, but too late. He tried, with journalistic cunning, to worm some news out of Vatanen and Kurko, but with no success. Kurko was helping Vatanen break up the last raft. The big winch had been taken away, and when the reporter asked if it was true that a hundred guns had been found in the river, Kurko chortled: 'A hundred guns! You must be daft. This is a raft-disposal not an arsenal.'

By Friday, the work on the rafts was complete and the two men were in Rovaniemi. Vatanen signed for his pay in the Forest Authority office, and Kurko sat impatiently in the downstairs room of the Lapland Restaurant. He'd been reckoning up the return on his business.

'The costs were 2,870 quid, counting in your five hundred. Ovako pay 8 pence a kilo at the works, and there were 96,000 kilos, or nearly a hundred tons. So reckon it up yourself. The whole shoot should be 768,000 pence: 7,680 quid! Take away 2,870 quid for costs and what am I left with? A cool four thousand eight hundred and ten quid. Tidy sum, that!'

In the afternoon the cheque arrived.

Kurko was so happy, he wept in the bank.

'I've not had a sum like that since 1964, when I did three months' solid felling at Kairijoki. Now, lad, I can be off . . . God knows where . . . Oulu even!'

Kurko left.

Vatanen decided to leave town, as there was an item in the *Lapland News*: legally, weapons the Germans left behind belonged to the Allies. An army major was reported as 'very surprised' to hear a rumour that 'private individuals' had salvaged war material left behind in the Lapland retreat and had allegedly sold it for their own gain.

Vatanen folded the paper and put it aside. He wondered where Kurko was now. No doubt he'd got himself some new false teeth.

'Shouldn't we be off too!' Vatanen asked the hare, who was sitting by his feet.

And so they left Rovaniemi behind. It was already well on into August. There'd been a little snow in the morning, but it had soon melted away.

13 The Raven

Before the snow set in, Vatanen took the bus to Posio in South Lapland.

There he took a forest-thinning job five miles from the highway that crosses the deserted forest tracts north of Lake Simojärvi. It was between the Kemijoki and Simojoki rivers, a desolate watershed, but the work brought money in, and the main thing was that the hare didn't have to live in a built-up area.

Vatanen established camp in a clump of red pines on a marsh islet at the edge of an extensive swamp. He lived in a lean-to canvas bivouac reinforced with a covering of spruce branches. Twice a week he went to Lake Simojärvi for food and cigarettes, and to borrow a few books from the local library. He spent several weeks in the Posio marshes, and he read quite a few good books during this period.

The conditions here, near the Arctic Circle, were very primitive.

The work was heavy, but Vatanen liked that: he knew he was getting stronger, and he wasn't weighed down by the thought of having to do this work till the end of his life.

Sometimes, as the sleet came down in the failing light of evening, and he felt very tired, he thought over his life: how different it was now from only last spring, in those days before midsummer!

Totally different!

He spoke aloud to the hare, and the hare listened religiously, without comprehending a word. Vatanen poked the camp-fire in front of his lean-to, watched the winter coming on, and at night slept with his ears pricked like a wild animal.

Right at the start, in this deserted and sleety marshland, he met a setback. While he was still fixing up his frugal camp between the little floating island's dried-up trees, the most villainous bird in the forest was settling in too – a raven.

Scrawny, it flew several circuits of the islet with sleet-drenched wings, then, noticing no harassment, settled on a tree near Vatanen and shook off the sleet like a rheumaticky dog. It was a most melancholy sight.

Vatanen looked at the bird and felt a profound compassion for it. Everything showed that the poor, ill-shaped fowl had not been having a very cheerful time of it recently: utterly wretched it was.

Next evening, coming back tired from the forest and getting ready to make his supper, Vatanen had a surprise. His knapsack, which had been lying open on the bivouac branches, had been plundered. A considerable amount of food had disappeared from it: half a pound of butter, practically a whole tin of pork, and many slices of rye crispbread. Obviously the culprit was that miserable flap-winged fowl that had aroused his sympathy the day before. It had clearly torn open the packaging with its bony beak, spilled the contents around and then spirited some off to a cache known only to itself.

The raven was sitting on the top of a tall pine, quite close to the bivouac. One side of the pine was covered with a shiny black mess: the raven had been shitting from its branch.

The hare was rather nervous: obviously the raven had been molesting it while Vatanen was away working.

Vatanen threw a stone at the raven but missed. It merely shuffled aside, not even opening a wing. It switched trees only when Vatanen ran at the tree with an axe and started chopping.

If only he'd had a gun.

Vatanen opened another tin of meat, fried it in the pan and ate the rest of the crispbread dry, without butter. As he ate his reduced repast, he eyed the raven on its branch and heard it burping.

An unassuageable black rage overwhelmed him, and before settling to sleep he moved the knapsack under his head. The hare hopped behind his head to sleep, sheltering close to the damp canvas of the bivouac.

In the morning Vatanen carefully closed up the bivouac entrance with spruce branches, hiding the knapsack inside after making sure the cord was tightly fastened.

When he returned in the evening, the camp had again been raided. The raven had knocked the branches aside, dragged the bag outside the charred circle of the camp-fire, torn one of the pockets open and eaten the 'Rapid-shooter's processed cheese. The bird had also snipped through the cord and gobbled up the contents of last-night's meat-tin, and, likewise, the rest of the crispbread. All that was left was a packet of tea, some salt and sugar, and two or three unopened tins of meat.

That evening supper was still more frugal.

The pillage continued for several days. The raven succeeded in pillaging the knapsack's victuals even though Vatanen covered it over with large pieces of log before setting off for work: the raven always managed to worm its beak through the cracks and get into the bag. The knapsack would have to be enclosed in a concrete bunker, if it was to be safe from the greedy bird's ravages.

The raven became cheekier and cheekier, seeming to know that the man in the bivouac had no way of stopping it. Try as he could to dislodge the bird with ferocious roars and stones as big as a fist, the raven remained unperturbed even a little amused by Vatanen's impotent rage.

The bird was rapidly putting on weight and hardly bothered to shift from its branch even in the daytime. Its insatiable appetite forced Vatanen to frequent the food-van three times a week instead of two. He worked out that the raven was costing him nearly thirty pounds a week.

This went on for two weeks.

The bird had become grossly fat. It sat lazily and impudently on a branch just a few yards away from Vatanen, puffed up, like a shaggy, well-fed sheep; its formerly greyish-black plumage had darkened and developed a prosperous shine.

At this rate, Vatanen's forest clearance would bring in a very poor return. He gave much cogent thought to ways of getting rid of the bird, and when the invasion had lasted a couple of weeks he hit on the ultimate contrivance.

The way to make the raven renounce its iniquitous behaviour would be exceptionally effective.

And cruel.

Vatanen made another food-trip to Lake Simojärvi. The girl in the food-van couldn't help looking askance at her odd customer: apart from turning up three times a week with a hare, he was buying more and more food each visit. Yet it was common knowledge he was buying food only for himself.

The word started to go round: 'There's this fantastic eater out there. Three times a week he's in. He buys a stack of food, and all he does is get thinner.'

The day after his brainwave, Vatanen opened a two-pound meat-tin in a new way: instead of cutting round the edge, he slit a cross in the top, forming four sharp tin-triangles. He carefully prised the points upwards so that the meat-tin resembled a freshly-opened flower with four metal petals. Vatanen dug the meat out of the centre of this corolla with the point of his sheath-knife, fried the meat and ate heartily. The raven eyed the goings-on with a detached air, clearly expecting the rest of the tin to be its own as usual.

After hurling his usual maledictions at the raven, Vatanen set to concealing his knapsack under the logs. Before doing so, however, he praised the triangular points back inside, so that the opening formed a kind of funnel, like the entrance to a lobster-pot.

As soon as Vatanen left for the forest, the raven flopped down by the dying fire and strutted over to the concealed knapsack. It turned its head on one side for a second and then energetically set to: it edged its beak between the logs, tore at the knapsack straps, croaked a comment or two, nudged the logs about and very soon pulled out its booty. Every now and then it lifted its large black head and cocked its eye to see if Vatanen was on the way back.

Having tugged the knapsack out, the raven dragged it a little farther off to a level spot where, during the previous two weeks, it had customarily carried out its predations. There, it opened the bag with an experienced twist and attacked the contents.

Vatanen was watching developments from the shelter of the forest.

The raven hooked a crispbread packet out of the bag, gobbled several fragments, then took a whole crispbread in its beak. It started running with the crispbread in its bill, beating the air with its wings. It resembled a fully-loaded transport aircraft about to take off from a short runway on an important mission. Its wings gathered air, and it rose from the ground. The hare backtracked into the bivouac in terror, seeing the pirate craft taking off.

The raven flew over Vatanen's head with the whole slice of crispbread in its beak. It was like a kite: the morning wind coming across the vast marsh took hold of the broad wafer, and the heavy bird needed all its strength to beat air and hold course towards its forest hide-out.

Soon the raven was back, and the hare, which had meanwhile managed to forage a little in the marsh grass, hid away in the bivouac. Vatanen watched more attentively.

The raven clopped the meat-tin out of the knapsack. Before examining the contents, it stretched up and eyed the surroundings to be sure the coast was clear. Then it thrust its big head into the depths of the tin.

The creature bolted down several gulps of the greasy meat at the bottom and then decided to come up for air.

But its head wouldn't come out. The raven was snagged.

It panicked. It bounced away from the knapsack, trying to wrench the tin off, but the snare remained obstinately stuck. The bird clawed in vain at the slippery sides of the tin, and the sharp metal edges sheared into its greasy neck.

Vatanen rushed over, but too late. The black looter took wing, making a great racket, the tin still tight on its head. It couldn't see its way but gained enough height to prevent Vatanen finishing it off on the spot.

It went cawing its distress inside the tin. The marsh rang with metallic kronkings, muffled but fateful. It flew sheer up like an evil black swan heading straight for Tuonela, the Land of the Dead. There was a clatter and rattle in the tin, and behind that the overwrought croaking of the bird.

All sense of direction lost, incapable of a straight trajectory, it was performing aerobatics. Soon it lost height and crashed into the highest tree-tops at the edge of the forest. The tin rattled against the branches, and the bird tumbled to the ground, only to fly up again, bleeding, to new heights.

Vatanen saw it disappearing across the forest. Nothing but fearful noises reached the camp-site, telling of the robber-bird's last journey.

A drizzle of sleet started, and soon the sounds stopped.

Vatanen picked up his ransacked rucksack, took it into the bivouac, hugged the hare in his arms and looked at the horizon, the edge of the forest. There was more raven's blood in the tin than meat, he knew, and there was enough cruelty in him to laugh out loud at his foul play.

And it looked as if even the hare might be laughing too.

14 The Sacrificer

The week after the raven's death, Vatanen left Posio marsh and went to Sodankylä, about ninety miles north of the Arctic Circle. Spending a few days resting at a hotel there, he met the chairman of the Sompio Reindeer Owners' Association, who offered him a job repairing a bunkhouse in Läähkimä Gorge in the Sompio Nature Reserve. It was just the thing.

He bought a rifle with a telescopic sight, skis, carpenter's tools and food for several weeks. He ordered a taxi and drove a hundred miles farther north along the Tanhua road into the wild forest land. At the Värriö fork he came across a group of reindeer herdsmen sitting round a fire at the roadside.

'Can't make it out,' said one. 'The hares round here have been white for weeks, while that one there's still in its summer coat.'

'Could be a brown hare.'

'Never, a brown hare's bigger.'

'It's a southern hare,' Vatanen explained. The taxi-driver helped him get his baggage out of the taxi. It was snowing somewhat, but not enough to ski yet.

The herdsmen offered Vatanen coffee. The hare sniffed the men's forest smell with curiosity, showing no fear.

'If Kaartinen sees that, he'll sacrifice it,' one of the herdsmen told Vatanen.

'Used to be a teacher, maybe a priest too in the south. He does that – sacrifices animals.'

This Kaartinen, it emerged, was still a youngish man, a skiing instructor at Vuotso. In late autumn, out of season, he tended to ski in the nature park and live in the bunkhouse at Vittumainen

Ghyll, near Läähkimä Gorge.

The herdsmen were still sitting by the fire as Vatanen hoisted his heavy equipment on his shoulders, took a look at the map and disappeared into the forest. The hare followed, hopping joyously. It was about twenty miles through the forest to Läähkimä Gorge. With only scanty snow, Vatanen had to carry his skis on his shoulder, and they tended to catch on the branches, slowing down his progress.

Darkness fell early; he'd have to kip down in the forest. He felled a pine, set up his bivouac and made a log-fire for the night. Then he cut a slice of reindeer meat into the frying-pan. The hare settled to sleep in the bivouac, and soon Vatanen was stretched out too. Large snowflakes floated into the fire, vanishing in the flames with a slight hiss.

On the morrow, Vatanen had a day-long tramp before he sealed his destination and could say: 'Ah! Läähkimä Gorge bunkhouse.'

He leaned his skis against the wall and went wearily inside. The log cabin was an ordinary reindeer-herder's bunkhouse, built in the old days as a base for men rounding up reindeer. The previous winter a snowmobile had delivered boards, nails, rolls of roofing felt, a sack of cement. The bunkhouse had two rooms; one end was almost a ruin, and even the better end had a rotten floor that would need replacing.

'I've got time enough for this, if it takes me till Christmas,' said Vatanen, talking to himself. To the hare he said: 'You'd better get your winter coat on. We're not in Heinola now, you know. A goshawk'll get you in that brown.'

Vatanen picked the hare up and examined its coat. When he plucked at the hairs. they came away easily. A clean winter white was coming up underneath. Good, Vatanen thought, and put his ruffled friend down.

Vatanen was in no great hurry to start work. For several days he wandered about the neighbourhood, seeing how the land lay, and bringing in wood for the fire. In the evening lamplight he planned the repair of the cabin.

There was a sandy ridge nearby, and he dug several sacks of fine sand out of the snow for bricklaying. With planks, he constructed a mortar-mixing trough. The first thing to put right was the fireplace, which was in the worst repair: it was important to be able to warm up the cabin, and the first really freezing temperatures came as he began mixing mortar. The chimney was equally dilapidated; it needed plastering, but that was difficult in the subzero temperature: the mortar froze instead of hardening.

Time is in abundant supply in the wilderness, and Vatanen decided to put it to good use. He went up on to the roof and built a sort of tent round the chimney-stack with his bivouac. Then he opened a space round the stack, going through both the roof and ceiling, so that warm air from inside the cabin rose into the tent. He put a ladder across the roof and carried steaming mortar up to the chimney.

While he was repairing the chimney-stack, a couple of reindeer-drivers ski'd up to the cabin. The snow was already thick enough to make skiing more practicable than walking. They were astounded at the weird-looking contrivance on the roof, and neither of them could work out why a tent had been put there. If their curiosity was stirred by this contraption, which was steaming slightly from its orifices, they were even more astonished to see the cabin door opening and a man carrying out a heavy, steaming bucket. He was so wrapped up in his job, he didn't notice the reindeermen leaning on their ski-sticks in the forecourt. He carried the heavy bucket up the ladder, picking his laborious way across the roof, giving himself a rest every now and then.

Once up, he disappeared inside the canvas cover and stayed there a good quarter of an hour. Finally he came out again, knocked the bucket against the edge of the roof to shake out the remains of the mortar and came down.

The reindeermen said: 'Morning.' They took their skis off and went inside.

In the middle of the floor stood Vatanen's mortar-mixing trough, some boards and various other building materials. They showed the reindeermen that nothing more remarkable was going on than repair of a chimney and a fireplace.

There was a fire burning in the fireplace, not interfering with the repair work, as the mortar dried better with the warmth. The reindeermen made some coffee on the fire. They were rounding up the remaining reindeer into the pound, they said: many herds had scattered in the forest. The construction of the Lokka artificial lake had meant less pasturage for the deer. It had messed the system up: now herding reindeer was much more difficult than before.

They had come via the cabin at Vittumainen Ghyll. Kaartinen, they said, had been living there.

They spent the night with Vatanen. After they'd gone, Vatanen was hard at work on the roof for a couple of days before the chimney was sturdy enough to last a few decades. When the mortar was dry he removed the chimney's tent. Then he swept the snow off the roof and began nailing new asphalt felt on top of the old worn-out stuff. The subzero frost made the felt stiff and difficult to handle without cracking it. Vatanen had to carry boiling water on to the roof and pour it over the felt veneer, standing on the ridge. The hot water softened the asphalt and, working quickly, he was able to spread the felt out smooth and nail it firmly to the roof.

It was a conspicuous activity: the boiling water steamed into the frosty air, enveloping everything, and floating high off in the clear sky. From a distance the site looked like a steam-driven power station or the kind of old-fashioned railway engine that swallowed water and puffed out steam. Vatanen resembled some engineer trying to get a huge engine going under freezing conditions. The blows of his hammer were like the knockings of an engine cranking up. But the bunkhouse was no machine, nor was it going anywhere. Once, straightening his back and waiting for the clouds of vapour to disperse. Vatanen's eye fell on the far slope of the gorge below. There were tracks leading up to the tangled thickets on the far gorge-side. Something had been walking there.

Vatanen got down from the roof, took his rifle and climbed back up. Now the steam had dispersed and he could see clearly through the telescopic sight. He pressed the gun to his cheek and took a long look at the opposite slope, occasionally giving his eye a rest. Finally, when his eyes were beginning to water, he lowered the weapon.

'It can't be anything but a bear.'

He went down into the cabin, ushered the hare in and started cooking. He pondered: now I've got a hibernating bear as a neighbour.

The hare fidgeted around the room. It always did that when it noticed its master had something on his mind.

At first light Vatanen ski'd across the gorge to look at the tracks more closely. The hare sniffed them and began to tremble with fear. No question, a bear had been there, and a big one. Vatanen followed the tracks to a treeless slope and farther on to a dense thicket of pines and fire. He ski'd a wide circle round the thicket but didn't see any emerging tracks. So the bear was in the thicket, and now he'd ski'd all the way round it. Quite clearly the bear had made a den for itself in the thicket and was sleeping heavily.

Vatanen ski'd into the thicket. The hare didn't dare follow him, even though Vatanen tried to coax it in a low voice. It remained on the open slope, looking insecure.

The bear had wandered about in the thicket, searching, no doubt, for a suitable lair. Difficult to know where it was. Vatanen had to ski deeper among the trees. Then he saw a tree that had been felled by the wind; the bear had crept under it. Not much snow had fallen on the lair as yet, and a little vapour was trailing up from under the tree-trunk. So that was where it was lying.

Vatanen silently turned his skis and glided out of the thicket on to the treeless slope, where the hare hopped joyously up to receive him.

Back at the bunkhouse, Vatanen realized he had a visitor. Factory-made cross-country skis were leaning against the cabin wall. Inside sat an athletic-looking young man in skiing clothes. He offered his hand in greeting – a somewhat odd custom in Lapland. It was Kaartinen, whom Vatanen had heard so much about.

Kaartinen was entranced with the hare. He tried to stroke it and pat it, and Vatanen had to ask him to stop, as the hare didn't like being petted. It was apparently shy of the man, though it didn't usually fear visitors if Vatanen was present.

Kaartinen said he was setting up a six-mile ski-trail from the cabin at Vittumainen Ghyll to here at Läähkimä Gorge. He produced two rolls of plastic tape from the inside pocket of his ski-jacket, one red, one yellow. He was going to use them to mark out a trail for tourists. A group of official visitors were coming for a backwoods holiday even before Christmas: that was the work of the Minister for Foreign Affairs. Several dozen VIP guests were coming, and the press too.

Kaartinen offered to buy the hare: first he offered twenty-five pounds, then fifty, and finally a hundred. Vatanen was certainly not going to sell: he was almost incensed at the ski instructor's offer.

Kaartinen stayed the night. Vatanen's thoughts were occupied with the bear, and it was quite a while before he got to sleep. When he did drop off, his sleep was all the sounder.

In the morning Vatanen woke to find himself alone. There was no sign of either the hare or Kaartinen. Kaartinen's skis were not outside, and there were no fresh hare-tracks.

How, why! In a rage, Vatanen leaped on to his skis, pushed off along Kaartinen's tracks, but came back almost at once. He lifted the gun off its nail, and started out again. What the reindeermen had said about sacrificing was going through his head. Vatanen went like the wind.

He swept up to Vittumainen Ghyll, puffing and blowing. He was in a sweat, steaming, his eyes smarting with sweat, and black rage was burning in his breast. By the Ghyll stood what was, in effect, a handsome country hostel, a log house big enough for a hundred people at least.

Vatanen kicked his skis off and wrenched the door open. Kaartinen was at a table by the window, just having coffee.

'Where's the hare!'

Kaartinen backed to the wall, staring in a funk at Vatanen, who was gripping a rifle in his fist. Terrified, Kaartinen stammered out that he knew nothing about the hare. He'd left so early: he hadn't had the heart to awaken his host, who was sleeping so soundly. That was all.

'You're lying! Give me that hare, and quick!'

Kaartinen fled into a corner. 'What would I be doing with it?' he protested.

'The hare!' Vatanen roared. When Kaartinen still refused to admit a thing, Vatanen completely lost control. He flung his weapon on the table, strode across to Kaartinen, grabbed him by the lapels and lifted him against the wall.

'Kill me if you like,' Kaartinen spluttered. 'You'll not get the hare.'

Vatanen became so enraged, he dropped the man from the wall, flung him into the middle of the room and gave him a cracking blow on the chin. The luckless skiing instructor went flying full-length across the cabin floor. There was silence, broken only by Vatanen's panting breath.

Another sound became audible. A faint scratching and quiet thumping was coming through the kitchen safety-vent. Vatanen ran outside, in through the kitchen door, and wrenched a cupboard door open. On the floor rolled a hare, its feet tied together, Vatanen's hare!

Vatanen cut the strings with his sheath-knife and returned to the other room with the hare in his arms. Kaartinen was just coming to.

'What's the meaning of this!' Vatanen demanded threateningly.

Then Kaartinen told his story: it was long, and not a little bizarre.

He had grown up, he said, in a very devout atmosphere: his pious parents were determined to bring their son up as a priest. When he passed his university entrance exam, he was sent to Helsinki University, in the theological faculty. But his studies there didn't chime with his sensitive youthful scrupulousness: he was not as convinced by the Lutheran doctrine as he ought to have been. Doubt gnawed at him; his theological studies seemed alien. It alarmed him to think that one day, himself troubled by scepticism, he'd nevertheless have to preach the word of God to the faithful. Thus, disregarding his parents' religious sentiments, he broke off his theological studies and enrolled at the Kemijärvi Teachers' Training College. There too he tangled with Lutheranism, but the presence of Jesus was not as overpowering. Kaartinen qualified as a primary-school teacher.

While still at the teachers' college, in a muddle of shifting notions about what was real, he hunted for his true identity in literature. He was fascinated by Tolstoyism, but the charm of that faded with time. Then he turned to oriental religions, particularly Buddhism, whose study went deepest with him. He was even planning a trip to Asia, to visit the centres of the faith, but his parents, who certainly weren't going to countenance pagan notions, refused travel money, and Kaartinen's oriental leanings gradually diminished through force of circumstance.

In his first and only teaching post Kaartinen became interested in anarchism. He ordered anarchistic French works for the Liminka school library and, with the help of a dictionary, pored over them. He put the ideas sufficiently into practice for the school authorities to relieve him of his duties at the end of the spring term. The following summer, no longer a teacher, he renounced his disastrous anarchistic ideology and enthusiastically immersed himself in ancient Finnish culture, in his own roots. He waded through dozens of works inspired by the exalted ideal of promoting Finnishness. That summer of study led him, as autumn drew on, into a deep insight into the prehistory of the Finnish people. The more he immersed himself in the thought-world of his forefathers, the more convinced he became that he'd finally found what he'd been feverishly searching for all those years: he'd hit upon the faith of his ancestors, the true religion of a true Finn.

Now he'd been practising his faith for years. In rapture, he expounded it for Vatanen. He told of forest spirits, earth spirits, the god of thunder, stone idols, the primal forest's shaman-seers, spells, sacrificial offerings. He introduced Vatanen to ancient religious rites and rituals and revealed that he himself had adopted the thousand-year-old sacrificial practices of his ancestors. Since becoming a northern skiing instructor, Kaartinen had enriched his Finno-Ugrian religious ideas with Lappish notions and, when alone in the wilds, he celebrated all those rites. Urban life, he said, made the practice of religion impossible.

Near the headwaters of Vittumainen Ghyll, at the edge of a little pond, he had carved his own fish-god, using a mechanical saw. It was a stone idol, resembling those of the Lapps. Outside the tourist seasons he worshipped it. At the centre of the god's sacred circle he had set up a sacrificial stone for burnt offerings. There, it was his practice to immolate living creatures, sometimes a Siberian jay trapped in a net, sometimes a snared willow-grouse, even a puppy bought in Ivalo. This time he had wanted to make an offering of a true wild animal from the forest − Vatanen's hare; and when Vatanen hadn't agreed to sell it, Kaartinen was left with a single way of propitiating his gods: he had to steal it from its master.

In his new life, he claimed, he was living a very rich, balanced and full existence. He felt the old gods were pleased with him, and that there were no other gods. He wished this same wonderful peace of mind for Vatanen; they should join forces, and, communing together, sacrifice the hare to the gods.

After this long account of Kaartinen's religious pilgrimage, Vatanen consented to overlook the incident; but he also insisted on Kaartinen swearing to stay well away from the hare in future, and particularly where his religious concerns were in mind.

When, that evening, Vatanen slowly ski'd back from Vittumainen Ghyll to Läähkimä Gorge, accompanied by his hare, he no longer thought about Kaartinen's strange world. There was a half-moon, and the stars were glimmering faintly in the frozen evening. He had his own world, this one, and it was fine to be here, living alone in one's own way. The hare ambled silently along the trail ahead of the skier, like a pathfinder. Vatanen sang to it.

15 The Bear

Vatanen felled several stout pines near the corner of the bunkhouse, sawed them to the right length, whittled them into building logs with his axe, hoisted the substructure of the cabin with a long lever, knocked out rotten logs and fitted the new ones in their place. A handsome wall resulted.

For the hare, he felled several aspens from a pondside and hauled them into the yard. The simple creature busied itself with them all day, as if it too had its building work to get on with. At any rate, the aspens turned white as the hare ate the bark.

Vatanen replaced a broken window with a new pane. He tore up the rotten flooring inside the bunkhouse and nailed new boards down. In between the two layers of the floor he poured the fine-grained contents of some abandoned anthills – a good insulation. The cabin at Läähkimä Gorge was looking splendid.

Scarcely a month after Kaartinen's visit, Vatanen again had visitors.

Ten soldiers ski'd into the yard – from the infantry battalion stationed at Sodankylä, they said. Brewing tea on the fire, the lieutenant in charge explained that the battalion was going to carry out a three-day military exercise in these Lapp backwoods. And soon.

'A bit taken aback ourselves we were. We've the Foreign Minister to thank for it. Wants some sort of a show for the foreign brass he's invited up for a Lapland trip. So it's full-scale battle manoeuvres, say-so of GHQ. Bloody foreigners: five hundred men shouting battle-cries in the forest about sod-all.'

The lieutenant asked Vatanen if the scheme's HQ could use the cabin at Läähkimä Gorge as their billet. The Foreign Minister's crowd were staying at Vittumainen Ghyll, he'd heard. 'So, is it all right if we come here?'

'Be my guest. Make yourself at home,' Vatanen agreed.

Two days before the official start of the exercise, a stream of soldiers began arriving at the Läähkimä bunkhouse. Some NCOs and several privates turned up on a snowmobile, bringing radio equipment, maps, food supplies, tents, unit flags. Vatanen asked if he could buy some ski-wax and pork off them, but the quartermaster said: 'No, help yourself, if you want.'

The next day more troops arrived. A long grey file of soldiers, conscripts, ski'd to the bunkhouse. The lads were worn out. Army trucks grumbled, tents billowed around the bunkhouse and down the gorge-side, and one tent was pitched almost at the bottom of the gorge.

Vatanen was afraid the din would waken the bear. He hadn't intended to speak about the bear to begin with, but now he told the major in charge of operations that if the troops weren't soon deployed towards Vittumainen-Ghyll, the bear might wake up, and Vatanen couldn't answer for the consequences.

'To hell with the bear. I've other things to think about. Read that book by Pulliainen, reindeerman. You'll see bears are nothing to get kittens about.'

In the night the temperature fell to more than minus twenty. Vatanen slept badly. He felt the hare breathing short sharp breaths by his ear: it seemed to be on edge too, poor thing.

And what Vatanen feared happened, very nastily.

In the early hours, about five o'clock, a group of soldiers burst into the cabin: they were carrying one of their comrades in a blanket. When the lamps were lit and the surplus men had been ordered out, the injury could be seen.

The lad was covered from head to foot in frozen blood. His right hand had been torn almost off. He'd fainted, probably through loss of blood. The MO was sent for; he bandaged the lad and gave him a tetanus jab. An army truck started up in the yard; the radio operator asked for a helicopter, but flight permission had not be granted. The chopper was reserved for the use of the Foreign Office.

The mauled conscript was wrapped in blankets and lifted into the truck. The bearers wiped their blood-stained hands on their trouser-legs as the truck began bumping off through the dark forest towards the nearest highway.

Shots rang out from the dark gorge. Vatanen went out and shouted in their direction: 'Quit shooting in the dark! You might hit it!'

Later in the morning, when it was light enough, Vatanen ski'd down into the bottom of the gorge. The soldiers told him what had happened.

The man on fire fatigue had gone to look at the bear-tracks by torchlight. He'd gone into the thicket, though the sentry warned him not to. A short time later the sentry saw the torch go out, heard a crashing and a yelling in the trees, and then nothing. When the men leaped out of their tents to help their comrade, a huge black bear with a white ring round its neck burst out of the thicket and ran into their lights. Spattering the men with snow, it fled into the darkness.

In the cabin the officers discussed what had happened and gave the situation some thought. They bleakly concluded that neither war nor military exercises depended on one casualty. The major decided to put the exercise in gear exactly as planned. Tents were dropped. Soldiers quietly ski'd off in single file for Vittumainen Ghyll, where, the following day, they were to give a demonstration of combat for the foreign military attachés.

A radio message came from the Foreign Minister's private secretary at Vittumainen Ghyll. News had reached them that a bear had been sighted at Läähkimä Gorge; the military attachés and their wives were extremely interested.

'We'd like to have a go at it. What we want is, first, to get a good look at it, photograph it, you know, and film it. Then shoot it. Can you arrange that?'

The major, who was receiving the call, objected. The bear, he pointed out, was dangerous: during the night it had mauled a man almost to death.

The private secretary dismissed the warnings. Clearly, the attachés had excellent weapons, and experience in using them. They all had the rank of colonel. The major was worrying needlessly.

'But in Finland bears are a protected species,' the major persisted.

'We've taken that into account. Been in touch with the Minister for the Environment. When he heard the bear had attacked one of your men, permission was granted.'

The major had to give in. He detailed a truck to bring the attachés and their wives on their bear-hunt. As daylight faded, a colourful party was driven over from Vittumainen Ghyll, including the Swedish,

French, American and Brazilian attachés, and two women: the wives of the Swedish and American attachés.

'This is something else!' the American attaché's wife rejoiced. 'Can you believe it? Shooting one of these black polar bears?'

The party could hardly wait for their dawn ski-trip and bear-hunt.

The HQ operations-room, with its radio equipment, was handed over to the women for the night. The major dejectedly took his equipment to a tent and directed night operations from there.

Milk cans were used to heat up water for the women to wash. Outside by the camp-fire, the soldiers tinkered with the boiling water and beefed about their assignment. Two pea-soup dixies were washed and consecrated to the women for more intimate ablutions. The dixies were modestly draped in towels.

'Blast!' the signals sergeant said. 'We forgot a mirror and a piss-pot!'

The problem was solved with a milk churn, delivered into the women's bedroom, The Foreign Minister's private secretary was delegated to explain the purpose for which it was reserved. The women looked at the churn and then enthused: 'Gee, talk about every contingency. The Finnish Army sure is well set up. These cans are really practical for field conditions! How come *our* armies don't have equipment like this!'

When both rear-mirrors had been screwed off the truck and handed over to the women, the Foreign Minister's private secretary was able to heave a sigh: the problems were pretty well straightened out now, even if conditions here *were* rugged.

In the morning a couple of conscripts were detailed to empty the milk-churns the women had used in the night. They carried the cans gravely out, but as soon as they were outside they ran into the forest and tipped them into the snow. They retched and laughed.

'Pipe down, you men!' the major called from the steps. 'And get those churns washed out, smart. I want to see sunshine coming through their sides.'

The bear's tracks were easily found. The hunting party was brought into single file. Vatanen ski'd off first, following the tracks. Next came the hare, then several officers, and finally the rest of the party. Vatanen was fairly convinced the hunt would come to nothing, and as far as he was concerned that was fine.

After an hour's skiing, the group had split up into a long broken queue: the military attachés, apart from the Brazilian, were still keeping up with Vatanen; the women and the other members must have stopped off somewhere farther back for coffee.

After another hour's smooth skiing, there came a surprise.

They came to the bear's former sleeping-place, and the bear was still there! It had dug itself a sort of den under the snow and was apparently sleeping down there. Vatanen hissed his discovery to the nearest men, and the word was passed along. The hare sensed danger again and ran around in terror at Vatanen's feet.

The group organized themselves into a firing position. Then they stood waiting for the women and the rest of the tail-end. About half an hour later the women staggered up, perspiring. The lady from the United States sat down on her skis in the snow and lit a cigarette. She was completely exhausted; the make-up from her eyes had run down her cheeks. She looked pretty miserable, and no mistake. Her Swedish sister was in better form, but she too was tired.

Vatanen entrusted the hare into the Swedish lady's arms and asked her to look after it for a while. Then he ski'd nearer to the lair. It was a weird feeling: he had butterflies in his stomach all right. There it was, the bear: exactly how fierce no one knew. Vatanen had not done anything like this ever before. He'd never hunted purely for pleasure. Now he was part of it, he felt both shame and fear.

Vatanen bellowed in horror. A film camera began to hum.

The bear woke with a jump but was at once alert to danger. It tossed the detritus aside and made a dash at Vatanen. Vatanen hit it on the head with the butt of his rifle, so hard he split the wooden butt. The bear darted through the cordon and turned to the women. Two shots rang out. Neither hit.

The bear reared in front of the Swedish lady and paused on its hind legs, apparently astounded at the sight of a woman hugging a hare in her arms. The bear sniffed the hare and then hugged the woman: three creatures in one embrace. The hare and the woman squealed with terror, alarming the bear. It hurled both of them away. They flew five or six yards, the hare still farther. And straight away the bear was off in full flight.

Several shots rang out after it. One may have hit, for the bear let out a great roar and turned towards its enemies; but then it continued its swift lope and had soon disappeared from sight.

A couple of soldiers ski'd off after the bear, though it now looked pointless. The rest of the party gathered round the Swedish lady, who was hysterical, weeping in the snow. Hardly surprising, after an ordeal like that.

They radioed for a jeep. A couple of hours later they were all back at Läähkimä Gorge. In front of the cabin there was a heavy air force helicopter; the women were helped into it. The Swedish woman had been holding on to the hare the whole time. Its coat was wet with her tears, and now she was taking the hare into the helicopter with her.

Vatanen objected.

'Come on now,' said the Foreign Minister's private secretary. 'You're a big man. Can't you see she's in a state of shock. You must let her hang on to it. . . . The Foreign Minister'll make it up to you. Anyway, you can get yourself a thousand hares in this forest, can't you?'

Vatanen refused to give up his hare. From the helicopter the lady sent word: she couldn't ever think of parting with the hare; it had shared the most scarifying moments of her whole life. The private secretary found himself anxiously negotiating under the helicopter blades in the bunkhouse yard. He tried a compromise, but his diplomatic skills weren't washing with Vatanen, they were getting nowhere.

The lady announced she could not, in any circumstances, leave this poor little hare in this fearful wilderness, a prey to wild beasts, at the mercy of savage Finnish men.

Vatanen proposed that if the lady could not, at the present moment, see her way to giving up what was not her property, the rights of the matter would no doubt be settled later.

'Very well, get in yourself,' the private secretary exploded, having had enough. 'You are, it must be said, an unusually petty-minded individual.'

The rest of the party climbed into the helicopter. The heavy warplane revved up its motors, lifted into the air and headed for Vittumainen Ghyll. There, a veritable winter war was in progress, but the foreign military attachés paid no attention to how things were going, They went straight from the chopper to the log hostel. Outside, the Finnish Army was left shouting battle-cries about . . . nothing.

16 The Dinner

In the spacious men's side of the Vittumainen Ghyll guest-house a table had been set for a magnificent dinner. The raw-pine long table had been covered with a handsome white cloth and loaded with succulent delicacies from Helsinki. Places for more than twenty had been set round the table. In the spaces between the delicacies stood bowls of fruit and miniature national flags of all the military attachés. The private secretary of the Foreign Minister presided at one end of the table, and a general from the Defence Staff at the other.

The bear-hunting women had gone off to change their clothes and now reappeared from the other and narrower end of the house. The hors-d'oeuvre was a choice fish canapé. Vatanen noticed that a couple of chairs were empty at the general's end of the table. He seated himself in one, for he was feeling hungry.

The private secretary gave Vatanen an angry look but said nothing. The officer from the Defence Staff, a major-general, gave Vatanen a soldierly greeting.

There was both rosé and white wine. Vatanen accepted the rosé. After the canapé, soup was served, a slightly gooey bisque extracted from tinned shrimps, but delicious.

The conversation turned to the day's happenings: in particular, the Swedish and American ladies were questioned endlessly about their bear-hunt. They went into detail, more especially the Swedish lady. The listeners sighed with horror at her ordeals and courage, and everyone was in ecstasies about her extraordinary luck. She also mentioned the hare, which by now had almost been forgotten. It was hastily produced and put into the lady's lap. She lifted the frightened animal on to the table-cloth and began to stroke it.

'I can never, in all my life, be parted from this adorable, brave creature! The bear would have killed me, I'm absolutely certain, if this poor innocent darling had not been in my arms.'

The major-general asked Vatanen if it was true that the hare was his. Vatanen said it was and whispered that he'd no intention of letting the lady have it as her darling.

'Might be a bit tricky getting it back now,' the general whispered.

The lady gave the hare some lettuce to eat, and it began eating voraciously. Its mouth went like a mill. A cry of delight went round the table. The hare was sharing a meal with the other members of the hunting trip! The company was audibly moved.

The general buzz alarmed the hare. It released a little cascade of pills on to the table-cloth. Some went into the Swedish lady's soup. The hare wriggled out of her hands and bounced along the centre of the table, knocking a candlestick over and leaving panicky droppings among the knives and forks.

The guests leaped to their feet: only the general and Vatanen remained seated. The general did pull his soup-plate on to his knees when he saw the hare hopping to his end of the table.

Vatanen grabbed the hare by the ears and put it on the floor, where the poor creature escaped into a corner. The guests seated themselves again. There was silence for a while.

The Swedish lady was more than a trifle on edge. Her left hand was fiddling with a lettuce leaf as if it were a napkin; she then sipped several spoonfuls of soup till she noticed the hare-droppings floating on the surface. She became still more uneasy, stared at her plate and then began delicately spooning the pills on to the rim, as one might dispose of some unwanted black peas in pea soup. Once the pills were on the edge of her plate, she gave a nervous smile, dipped her spoon a couple of times, but without appetite, and then suddenly dropped the spoon on to the table-cloth. She wiped her mouth with a lettuce leaf and said in embarrassment: 'Oh, how stupid of me . . . may I have another plate of soup, please.'

Her plate was removed. The hare droppings on the table were discreetly swept off, and a new cloth was spread. While all this was going on, a glass of vermouth was offered.

Then the dinner was resumed. The conversation seemed to be

eschewing the hunting episode. The Swedish lady did not even toy with her fresh soup: she stared at her plate, saying something inconsequential to her neighbours from time to time. And so it was the turn of the main dish. It was hare. What a coincidence!

The hare was delicious, but not many took a second helping: the situation was too ambiguous. Pudding was hurried along – arctic cloudberries in whipped cream – and then people rose from the table. The cloth was removed, coffee was served, with liqueurs and brandy, and only now did the atmosphere begin to relax.

Through the window soldiers could be seen skiing past in all directions; army trucks were grumbling across the twilit landscape. The guests looked out with bored stares: it was as if the window were a television screen someone had forgotten to switch off during a tedious programme. Soon there was darkness outside, as if something were wrong with the tube: the picture slowly dimmed until complete blackness prevailed. Only the sound was still working: the battle-cries of the charging soldiers, the muffled reports of the blank cartridges, and the rumblings of the vehicles. The sounds penetrated the log walls of the Vittumainen Ghyll guest-house, where the VIPs chatted urbanely about this and that.

17 The Fire

At bedtime, Vatanen was settling down with his hare and his knapsack to sleep on the floor of the men's side of the Vittumainen
Ghyll guest-house, when the private secretary appeared and said:
'As I see it, you're rather out of place here . . . Mr Vatanen, as
your name is, I think. . . . I suggest you take yourself off with that
damned hare of yours, and don't put in an appearance again. That
is undoubtedly the best solution for all concerned. I've spoken to
the Swedish attaché, and he's of the same opinion. He tells me his
wife is no longer so set on retaining the hare as she was yesterday.'

Vatanen began collecting his gear.

'I do find it a little astonishing that you were able to bring yourself
to take a place at the official dinner. Was that a deliberate act?
And the animal, please get it out of here. It's already caused more
harm than you can imagine.'

'But it was the lady who decided she couldn't do without it,'
Vatanen muttered.

'It was your damned hare that caused all the trouble. And don't
permit yourself to refer to the lady or what she wants. Now get
yourself off. Here's fifty pounds, or a hundred, if you like. I want
to get this business completely off my hands.'

Vatanen accepted the notes and asked: 'Do your require a receipt?'

'Be off now, for God's sake.'

Vatanen had sorted out his gear. He slipped the hare into his
knapsack, its head poking above the top. Before going to the door,
he offered his hand to the official, who merely sucked his breath
in through his teeth angrily. Outdoors, Vatanen followed a path to
the end, and then went a couple of hundred yards or so farther, to

some soldier's tents. He climbed into a platoon tent and found a place to curl up and sleep. The weary soldiers were making tea and offered Vatanen a mug. No one asked any questions. The lad on fire duty threw more wet birch logs into the black stove, and someone moaned in their sleep.

In the small hours an alarm sounded, but no one left the tent. Someone dug out a pack of cards. Vatanen perked up at that and said he'd make the running – if anyone wanted a game?

He plonked the hundred pounds on the blanket, saying where it had come from, and the whole tent joined in a poker game. An hour later the money had got around a bit. A soldier took a turn outside and came back with the news that one of the diplomat's wives had been sipping hareshit soup the evening before.

An order came through that camp had to be struck by six o'clock.

No one made the slightest move to carry out the order. In the dark outside, some night assault was evidently under way. The contribution of the men in the tent to the war-game outside was to yell assault-cries at the tops of their voices. The war was still going on: vehicles started to rumble and roar; tired shouts came from somewhere.

Around nine o'clock Vatanen emerged from the tent. It was still more or less dark, but the war-games had now livened up somewhat – enough, at any rate, to put a stop to the tent-life. Nevertheless, the tent had still not been struck.

That was perhaps as well, for the Vittumainen Ghyll guest-house was up in flames. It had evidently caught fire quite a bit earlier, and the flames were now out of control. The sleepers had woken up, and the windows were being blown out by the flames. Military men in underclothes, and their wives, were crowding out of the log building; shouting was getting vociferous. Very lights were shooting up in the air; the conscripts' war had taken second place.

Vatanen parked his knapsack, with the hare in, on the branch of a tree and dashed over to the building. The forecourt was crowded with people wrapped in blankets, bemoaning the crisis in a babble of different languages. The fire had probably started in the kitchen, for the centre of the kitchen roof had caved in, but the fire had now spread to the whole building. The major-general had taken charge: he was standing in stockinged feet in the middle of the chaos, bellowing out orders. He kept picking up one foot after the other: the snow was melting under his socks. He was wearing army trousers, but he had no tunic. In spite of that, everyone knew he was a general all right.

People were still jumping out of the narrow end of the house, including women, panicking and screaming. Vatanen recognized many of them, one especially: someone was leading the Swedish lady out of the smoke into the forecourt. She was naked in the frozen snow, weeping bitterly. The blazing flames threw her figure into silhouette, and she looked extremely beautiful picking her way through the snow supported by two soldiers; then a blanket was thrown round her. The whole building was now a mass of flames; soldiers were shovelling snow in through the windows, but someone swore it was going to melt the helmets on their heads.

The helicopter was standing at the verge of the forecourt and looked in danger of bursting into flames. The general bellowed for it to be taken away. Where was the pilot? A naked man ran to the helicopter, burned his hand as he touched the metal side, but managed to worm in, lowering the windows and shouting: 'Too cold! Can't take off yet!' His naked body was visible in the window, and sparks from the shell of burning logs were flying against the chopper's hot-metal sides like pine-cones in a storm.

The window shut as the general yelled: 'Up with it! Come on! Get a move on!'

The private secretary ran into the forecourt, he too half dressed. He asked the soldiers for jackets and shoes. Soon his arms were piled with clothes and boots, which he spread on the melting snow and distributed to the naked women covered in nothing but blankets. One woman received a pair of boots, another socks; tunics and greatcoats were thrown over the women's shoulders, till they were fat as queen bees; white camouflage hoods came down to their white shoulders.

The battalion sixth company came up at the double. Exhausted, they stopped at the edge of the melting snow. An officer bawled, but it was a very ragged semicircle the men formed round the burning building. Their stained white snowsuits flickered red in the blaze of the fire. The lads' faces, black and frost-bitten, looked improbable, hardly human; they were more like a chain of Moomins sent to close off the area. 'Got a match?' someone asked. A cigarette lighter circled from hand to hand, as the soldiers leaned on their ski-sticks.

The heavy army helicopter began thumping and throbbing, and soon there was a full-throated hammering, as the great blades be-

gan slowly churning the burnt air. Doubled up, the general ran
over to the flight cabin, signalling that people ought to be taken
along. The private secretary, realizing what he meant, began leading women to the juddering chopper. Vatanen resorted to the tree
and collected his knapsack off the branch, whispering soothingly
to his hare, which was frantic at hanging so long on a branch, in a
bag, in all this pandemonium.

Vatanen tossed the knapsack on his back and returned to the
scene of the fire. The hare whined in its bag but made no further
efforts to escape, and, in any case, the cord would have stopped it
if it had tried.

The private secretary led some women under the helicopter blades;
the door opened, and hands pushed on the women's bottoms, thrusting them, wrapped in thick army clothes, into the cabin. The helicopter pilot and his number two, stark naked at the door, were
giving a hand to help them inside. The general lit a cigarette. Vatanen
decided to go and help with the loading too. He jumped into the
machine and lifted struggling people in till the helicopter captain
said to him: 'That's it, lieutenant. We're off. Not a single one more.
Door closed!'

Lieutenant!

Vatanen was about to get back out, but the naked electronics engineer grabbed his arm, fastened the door in his face and clapped ear-
phones on: 'OH 226, OH 226, over. . . . Do you hear me? About to
be airborne. Destination Sodankylä Garrison Hospital. OK, Roger, out.'

The helicopter's windows were spotted with condensation, but,
giving the nearest window a wipe with his hand, Vatanen saw the
heavy blades starting to flash round with accelerating force. That
sent a new blast of wind into the burning building, and the furnace
spouted up ninety feet high. The tempest the helicopter was stirring grilled the collapsing log storeys to a new brightness: in the
pale morning light they glowed like Bengal lights. Then the machine became airborne.

From the ground, the general was sending airport hand signals:
he spread his arms and closed them at intervals. The people down
there were getting farther and farther off, and the ears of those in
the cabin were being dinned by the drumming. Soon the figure of
the general, standing in his braces, became very small; the glowing
building diminished, and the machine rose so high the sun blazed
into view.

Ah, what a sight!

Vatanen took the bag off his back and moved it round to the front; he pushed the hare's muzzle to the window, showing it the grandiose landscape.

'Look, boy, look.'

The hare looked, sighed and then huddled against its master's chest; it tucked its legs together in the bag, crouched into a foetal position and went off to sleep.

Immediately bright lights went on in the cabin. The cockpit door opened, and there stood a naked helicopter captain:

'We're on our way to Sodankylä. Flight time twenty minutes. I ask you to please keep calm. And then . . . could anyone lend me a little clothing.'

He was given a haphazard collection of items. Meanwhile the equally haphazard collection of people, about twenty of them, began taking a closer look at each other and peeping out of the windows. Vatanen noticed that opposite him was the private secretary, sitting tightly squeezed between two women, and looking distinctly ill at ease. When the official realized who was sitting opposite him, he said quietly, in a voice resigned to adversity: 'You here too. I might have guessed.'

He had no shoes. His bare feet were obviously icy. Vatanen took his shoes off and offered them to him, saying: 'Here, take these. Go on.'

The American military attaché's wife, who was sitting next to the official, noticed the hare; she pointed to it and said sweetly: 'What an adorable creature! How lovely it is! And always with us! May I stroke it?'

The helicopter was heading almost straight into the sun; the snowy wilderness was speeding by underneath. Back at Sompio, thick clouds of smoke could still be seen by a craning of the neck. The deserted forest glided vibrating below them. As they flew over Läähkimä George, Vatanen could see the tracks left by the bear-hunt. Nearer to Sodankylä he caught sight of a solitary figure plodding far below after a long trek: the tracks were like a mouse's, but the maker of them was black, and the direction south-east. Vatanen looked so hard, his eyes began watering. He came to the definite conclusion that it was Läähkimä Gorge's bear: it couldn't be anything else.

He said nothing. He brushed the drops from his eyes and stroked the hare. The smoke of Sodankylä was coming into view.

18 To Helsinki

The helicopter touched down in the forecourt of Sodankylä Garrison Hospital. It was quite a spectacle when the diplomats disembarked into the snow wearing their heterogeneous medley of borrowed clothes. A doctor came to receive them and shook each person by the hand, including Vatanen. The arrivals were ushered into a ward and given a medical examination.

The last one off was a naked airman. He lurked behind the chopper till, having made sure most of the women had gone into the hospital, he made a dash for a handy welfare centre. The doctor ordered clothes to be sent over to him: they'd been indented for.

Vatanen sat in the waiting-room with his hare and his knapsack. Soon various civilian clothes, shoes, underclothes, everything, arrived in a delivery van from Mannermaa, the department store. Everyone could select what he needed from the mounting pile on the waiting-room floor and go away to try them on. The private secretary picked out suitable footwear for himself and then returned Vatanen's shoes, thanking him.

Once his shoes were on, Vatanen left the waiting-room and hitched a lift to the high street in the Mannermaa delivery van. The driver had heard the news on the radio and asked Vatanen so many questions he began to feel weary.

Vatanen was fed up to the back teeth with the recent days' happenings. He got himself a hotel room and rang up the chairman of the Sompio Reindeer Owners' Association.

'I don't suppose the Läähkimä Gorge bunkhouse went up in flames too, did it?' the chairman said.

'No. But listen, it's time to pay me off now. I think I must be on my way. There wasn't much peace and quiet up there in Sampio, after all, you know.

'I believe you. Sure I'll settle up with you.'

The hare didn't look very well. It lay in the bag looking out of sorts, and when Vatanen let it out into the room, it hopped listlessly over to the bed and closed its eyes.

Vatanen rang the Sodankylä vet to ask what might be wrong. The vet came and examined the hare but couldn't say one way or the other.

'These wild animals can be funny, you know. Tamed, they can die for no special reason. Maybe that's the case now. The only place that might be able do anything for it would be the National Institute of Veterinary Science. They could analyse some blood samples – if they thought it worth their while, that is. But you'd hardly want to go all the way to Helsinki for the sake of a hare, would you? And, of course, they don't provide a private service.'

But, with the hare in such poor condition, Vatanen was determined to do anything he could to get it better. He managed to sell all the equipment he'd left behind at Läähkimä Gulf, including his skis, to the Sompio chairman, He hired a taxi to Rovaniemi and took the flight to the Seutala airport at Helsinki. At Seutala, he took a taxi direct to the National Institute of Veterinary Science.

Vatanen walked along the institute corridors without arousing any attention: for once he was in a place where a man wasn't stared at for carrying a hare.

With no difficulty, Vatanen found his way to a research professor's office; he pressed the bell-push by the door, and when the green light showed, carried his hare in.

Shuffling papers at his desk, sat a white-coated, oddly grubby-looking man, who rose to his feet, shook Vatanen's hand, then invited him to sit down.

Vatanen said he needed help, or rather the hare did, because it was poorly.

'So what's this hare, and what's the matter with it?' the professor said, taking the hare in his lap. . . . 'Hm, it might well have some parasite, I think. It couldn't have been in contact with some foreigners, could it? Or eaten some unwashed vegetables?'

'It could well have,' Vatanen said.

'It'll have to have some blood tests, then we can tell.'

He wrote an admission note on a yellow chit and handed it to

Vatanen, adding: 'The hare's from Evo, of course.'

Vatanen nodded.

He took his note to a laboratory and gave it to an assistant, who produced several hypodermic needles and took two or three samples from the trembling hare. The assistant said the results would be available in a couple of hours.

Vatanen went for a meal in the meantime and was allowed to leave the hare behind while the results were coming. A couple of hours later, Vatanen had more than a hare on his hands: a mass of papers, forming a sort of case history. He carried the documents back to the professor's study.

'As I expected,' the professor said. 'Intestinal. A couple of injections'll do the trick. I'll make out a prescription, and you can take the medicaments with you to Evo.'

The hare was inoculated, and Vatanen was given several ampoules and disposable needles.

'Something attempted, something done,' the professor said and took off his white coat. It was five o'clock.

'I'm driving to town. Come along, if you like, if you haven't a car with you.' The grubby professor was being most amiable. Vatanen got into the car, and the professor headed for the city centre.

'It should have lots of fresh water, but nothing to eat for two days. Then it can be fed as before. It'll certainly recover. I can drop you off at the train on my way, if you like – you did come by train, didn't you?'

Vatanen couldn't help replying: 'I came by plane, actually.'

The professor was nonplussed, then gave a laugh. 'But there's no plane from the Evo Game Research Institute!'

'I came from Rovaniemi, in fact – and before that from Sodankylä.'

'Not from Evo! But what . . .!' the professor said, completely disorientated.

Vatanen began to tell his story. He pointed out that the hare was indeed from the south, though from Heinola not Evo. Then he described his travels round Finland with the hare: Heinola, Nilsiä, Ranua, Posio, Rovaniemi, Sodankylä, Sompio, back to Rovaniemi, and now here. The professor had drawn the car up opposite the Sokos store in the midst of the Mannerheim Road rush-hour traffic. Parked by the pavement, he was listening to Vatanen with obvious disbelief. From time to time he put in with 'Impossible.'

When Vatanen had reached the end of his story, the professor said sternly: 'Excuse me, sir, but I don't believe a word of it. Quite a yarn, I admit, but why you're spinning it I can't imagine. Now take that hare back to the Game Research Institute, and I'll ring there in the morning.'

'All right, if you don't believe me, ring. I don't attach any importance to the stories.'

At Sokos corner a tired reindeer was tugging and pulling at its lead, while a broken-down old Father Christmas gave it a nasty kick on the hoofs. The reindeer kept its eyes closed, probably with pain. The deer was surrounded by squalling children, whose tired mothers were having to repeat again and again: 'Jari, Jari, stop trying to get on its back! Come on, Jari. Jari, listen. . . .'

Vatanen began to feel profoundly depressed. He begged the professor to drive on. The car turned down towards the station.

Stopping again, the professor said: No, I must relieve you of that animal. It won't do. I can't imagine who made you responsible for it. Now go back there. I'll send a man to Evo with it tomorrow. Tonight, I'll look after it myself, at home.'

He was not someone from the Evo Game Research Institute, Vatanen insisted.

'Look, this is not a trifling matter,' the professor said and made to take the hare. The car, parked by the snack-bar, was causing an obstruction.

Vatanen held on to his hare; but it was getting like the tale of the chalk circle: two women are pulling on a child by its arms and legs; the one who pulls the most ruthlessly wins the tussle; but the child really belongs to the one who lets go. Vatanen let go. His thoughts went to the permit. Where was it? Somewhere in the bunkhouse at Läähkimä Gulf. Then he said: 'I've a suggestion. Ring the vet in Sodankylä. That'll settle it. I'll pay for the call.'

The professor pondered for a moment. 'Very well, let's see. My flat's quite near, in Kruununhaka. I'll telephone from there. I don't in fact believe you, and you'll find you can't trifle with a hare. I love animals. They can't be left in just anyone's hands.'

'Yet you perform vivisection.'

'That's science. Nor is it your concern. It's my profession.'

The call was made. The Sodankylä vet confirmed Vatanen's story as far as the morning consultation in the Sodankylä hotel. He was amazed, however, that the person concerned had already proceeded to Helsinki.

Slowly, the professor put the receiver down. He gave Vatanen a very quizzical look. How much did the call cost? Vatanen asked. The professor seemed not to hear. He said: 'I'd like to hear your story once again. I'll make us a sandwich. You're not in a hurry, are you?'

'Not particularly.'

19 *Crapula*

He became aware he was lying on the floor, rolled up in a carpet. He was bilious: acid griped his stomach, came up into his throat, and he felt like vomiting. He didn't dare open his eyes; he heard nothing, but, putting his mind to it, he could detect all sorts of sounds: borborygmi, whistlings, singings in the ears. Again a yellow bile gushed into his mouth.

He lay still. The slightest motion, he knew, and he'd puke. He gulped back the bile. He didn't dare move enough to put his hand to his forehead, but he knew it was bathed in sweat.

He must smell vile, he thought. His explored his mouth tentatively: a thick tongue encountered a palate coated with glue.

And his heart? It did seem to be beating, though rather arbitrarily. His pulse was sluggish, like the plod of a bored sentry; but occasionally it put on a spurt: it gave a couple of enthusiastic biffs that almost burst his chest and reached his toes; then it stood stockstill a few seconds, totally arrested, spanked out a few short clouts, and then continued its sluggish plod. He had to take a tight grip on the carpet: the floor had taken off, and he was floating round the room; drops of sweat trickled down his neck; suddenly he felt feverish; the mat was weighing insufferably on his sweaty torso.

If only I dared open my eyes, one of them at least, he ventured, but opened neither. Even the thought seemed rash. He ought to try and go back to sleep: oh to sleep, to sleep till he was dead. But perhaps he was dead already? The thought made him want to laugh, though the mirth died instantly. Bile had again flushed into his mouth; it had to be manfully swallowed back.

He made an effort to grasp where he was in his life at the moment.

He couldn't grasp anything specific: possibilities, images flashed by, quite a few, but the brain couldn't get its teeth into them: not deep enough to call the result a thought.

At times this pursuit of thought struck him as a great joke. What was funny about it he couldn't quite make out; but something completely hilarious there was. Yet when he tried to concentrate on his weird hilarity, gloom took its place, and the gloom seemed only too well founded.

Everything was shifting about, everything slipping out of mind. For a second he thought of his head as a hand, withdrawing everything. My head's gliding away, he thought. The thought tickled him again, only for a moment; then oblivion fell. He decided he'd better turn his mind to something practical.

For instance, what time of the year was it? That was something to put one's mind to. A question like that would be distanced enough and yet practical. What season was it? Could you remember something like that, if you made a big effort?

Without realizing it, he'd opened his eyes. Concentrating on the season of the year had done what he'd been guarding against, and no particular harm seemed to have occurred. His gungy eyes focused on the wall near the ceiling. There was a large window, with eight panes: four small ones at the bottom, two larger ones in the middle, and two round-topped ones higher up; bright, though; he had to close his eyes. His eyelids were like the hatches of a diving-bell, he decided, and he determined to go back to pondering what time of the year it was.

Spring? Spring seemed to have some allure and rang a bell. But why not, just as well, autumn, or January...? No, not January, that rang no bell. Not summer either. Spring, though, made him think of a leveret, and that made him think of a bigger hare, his own... and that suggested autumn. Autumn made him think of Christmas; and now it felt almost like spring – March, most likely.

On further reflection, March didn't feel right either. More likely it was the fag-end of winter.

Nausea rushed back. He barricaded a disgusting fluid behind his teeth, burst out of the carpet, saw two other sleepers on the floor, realized that the lavatory door was straight in front of him and rushed in.

He threw up, stertorously; retching, the contents of his stomach fetched into the lavatory bowl; he dribbled slobber; his eyes popped;

his stomach contracted like a cow's after giving birth, then made as if to come out of his contorted mouth, with his heart banging his head off.

And then suddenly the nausea was over: a delicious confidence in the indomitableness of his system came back like a refreshing shower. He raised a purple face to the mirror and stood looking.

It was a coloured page torn from a porn magazine. He washed the sweat off it, bared his upper body, and washed his chest and armpits with a cold flannel. He found a comb in his pocket and ran it through his thick, matted hair. The hairs stuck to the comb. Pulling them away, his stiff, awkward fingers pulled several teeth out of the comb. He threw the lot into the lavatory bowl, gargled several times, then flushed the whole mess into the sewerage. When he opened the bathroom door and returned to the room, he remembered with astonishing clarity who he was, remembered it must be Christmas, but found recent happenings a complete haze.

The room was small, tidy too, clearly a dentist's surgery: chrome chairs and drills glistened in the sun flooding through the window. He sat down on a sofa by the wall, hands dangling between his knees like a farm labourer's, and took a look at the two other people lodging here like himself in this odd set-up.

One of them was a young woman, the other a middle-aged man. They had woken and piled up by the wall the sofa cushions they'd been using as beds. Vatanen greeted them. Both seemed familiar, yet so unfamiliar. He couldn't bring himself to ask where he was and who the other two were. He supposed time would clear these mysteries up.

The young woman, for she was more than a girl, clarified matters by saying the taxi ought to be paid off, so the driver could finally leave: two hundred and twenty-two pounds. Vatanen felt in his back pocket: his wallet had gone. The woman produced it from her handbag and handed it to him. The wallet contained a large wad, over nine hundred pounds. Vatanen counted out two hundred and thirty pounds and gave it to the woman. She gave it to the man, who thanked her and handed back eight pounds. So the man was a taxi-driver, Vatanen concluded.

'Goodbye, then,' the man said as he left. 'Quite a time of it we had. Cheers.'

'Take these,' the woman said, handing Vatanen some red vitamin pills from her handbag. 'They'll do you good. Just swallow them whole.'

Vatanen managed to ask where the hare was.

'No need to worry. It's safe in Helsinki, with some prof. It was left there before Christmas and can stay till New Year. It's all fixed up.'

'Before Christmas? Is it after Christmas?'

'Yes, yes, don't you remember?'

'I've got a bit vague about things. I must have been drinking a bit.'

'A bit more than a bit,' she said matter-of-factly.

'It feels like that. Who are you?'

'Leila. You could at least remember that!'

Vatanen began to recall the name Leila . . . of course, this woman was Leila. But what Leila? That he didn't dare ask just then but said: 'Well, it *is* coming back, don't be angry. But I've got this fearful hangover, it's affecting my memory, it seems. I must have been drinking for days. It's not my way, you know.'

'Alcohol poisoning. Now you've got to put the stopper on.'

Vatanen was horribly ashamed. He avoided her look, which was only too frank and honest. He glanced down at the floor, letting his eyes wander, and then a completely new thought struck him: 'Could we go somewhere and have a glass of cold beer, perhaps?'

Leila nodded, and they left.

The staircase was spiral, and they were three storeys up – six landings. Vatanen supported himself on the curved banister – the steps were dancing – and Leila supported his other arm.

Outside, there was a glaringly bright, frosty day. The sunny street was white with clean new snow. The dazzle made his eyes ache, but the fresh air perked him up a little. Shielding his eyes with his hand, he said: 'I'm an olm coming out of its cave.'

'A what?' Leila asked.

'Nothing. Take me somewhere nice.'

Leila led Vatanen across town. He observed the houses, the cars, trying to work out where he was. Vallila, was it? Katajanokka? Kruununhaka, anyway, it couldn't possibly be. They came to a river. . . . Was it Porvoo? No, not Porvoo. He knew Porvoo well.

Vatanen was feebly watching the passers-by, hoping, he realized, to see a face he knew, perhaps hear where they were, get himself back on the map.

They crossed a bridge: their destination was a little restaurant on the other side. It looked rather smart, and Vatanen didn't believe it could be open so early in the morning. He said so, and Leila pointed out it was afternoon already: 'You really are pretty fazed, aren't you?'

Vatanen glanced dully through the menu: he didn't dare think of eating. Leila ordered a frosted Pilsener for him and a glass of fresh fruit-juice for herself. He cautiously sipped the cold beer; its smell was sickening, but on the other hand it was stimulating. The first drop upset his stomach a little. He'd have to sit it out and see what happened.

Leila watched his silent struggle.

And then the power of the hangover was broken: it was thanks to the beer. Vatanen found himself able to eat. He became a new man, a new Vatanen.

He began to remember things and even remembered leaving his hare in the professor's flat in Kruununhaka and then going off for a binge, after half a year's abstinence. And he'd drunk in splendid style, drunk deeply and joyously. But he could remember only the early phases of the booze-up: events didn't become clear till Leila outlined their main course.

Her tale was as long and winding as the trip itself, which had lasted eight days and meandered through various southern Finnish venues. Vatanen had been up to a thing or two, quite a thing or two.

Warily, he slipped in: 'What town are we in now?'

'This is Turku,' she said.

'Ridiculous, not knowing!' he said. 'So that's why the bridge seemed familiar. I've been here dozens of times, but the sun was blinding me.'

Bit by bit the trip began to piece together, as Leila's story unfolded. Vatanen had binged in Helsinki for a couple days, had got into a fight, had been taken to the police station but was released straight away. He'd then met Leila, and they'd gone to Kerava, where one thing after another had happened, including Vatanen's falling under a train. The train had pushed him twenty yards along the track at walking speed, and he'd got away with bruises.

At Kerava Vatanen had bought a bicycle and pedalled off in a rage – some drunken fit of the sulks – towards Riihimäki. Leila had followed in a taxi. Vatanen had not reached Riihimäki on his bicycle: a patrol car had stopped him. The bicycle had been loaded into the taxi's boot and driven to Riihimäki, where it was sold at a knock-down price, and the money splashed on lottery tickets.

Vatanen had won a hi-fi set, a leather brief-case and pencil-case, cuff-links, a set of fountain-pens, and three leather memo-pads. He took the money instead and got it into his head to bus to Turenki, which they did.

In Turenki they spent the night at a farm. Vatanen, whooped it up with cheerful abandon – even if it looked physically and spiritually wearing to Leila – and he was one of the village sights for three days.

On the day before Christmas Eve they left Turenki for Janakkala to spend Christmas with Leila's parents. Vatanen bought fine presents for all her family: a barometer for her mother, a selection of pipes for her father, a bracelet for her sister, and a xylophone for the youngest girl. On Christmas Eve Vatanen was charming: the family listened fascinated to his stories; Daddy produced his best brandy from the sideboard, and it went down well. Vatanen tended to drone on during the night and kissed Leila and her mother on their cleavage; but no one had been offended.

Christmas night they left Janakkala unexpectedly, supposedly for the hospital, but they didn't go there. Instead they took a taxi to Tammisaari, where Vatanen tried to take a Christmas dip in the sea, without success. They spent Christmas night sleeping in a taxi, which turned out to be expensive.

They also went to Hanko and Salo, where nothing particularly unusual happened. And now they were in Turku. They'd arrived in the middle of the night, and Vatanen had gone through the list of dentists in the directory, asking for an appointment, and one had accepted. The Hanko taxi-driver had spent the night in Turku. Throughout all this, Leila had been with him, and that astonished Vatanen.

'How on earth could you put up with all that?'

'It was my Christmas holiday, darling.'

Darling? Vatanen gave the young woman a second look: that put a different complexion on things. Did they have some sort of liaison? If so, what exactly?

She was certainly attractive, no question. Or rather, just that raised a question: how could a young woman as attractive as Leila endure this crazy trail of tomfoolery for so long? Surely, as a foul-smelling drunk, he hadn't had the indecency to seduce her? That would be difficult to believe, because, judging from her account, his behaviour had been revolting from beginning to end.

Besides, she was apparently engaged, he observed. A ring glinted on her finger: cheap and nasty, a sort he personally wouldn't want to buy for any woman, let alone a woman of this quality. For a moment he had managed to think something lovely might have happened, something inconceivable, between this travelling companion and himself; but the hideous ring put a stop to that.

He was overwhelmed by a feeling of loneliness: even his hare was in Helsinki. He suddenly felt an unbearable yearning for his hare.

'I must go and get that hare,' he said sadly, looking at the ring. 'You're engaged, I see, and I can't help saying I don't think much of the ring.' He sighed deeply.

'Guess who I'm engaged to,' she said, looking him gravely in the eye.

'Oh, some high-flying young accountant, I suppose. Forgive me, but it doesn't interest me.'

'Wrong . . . . Guess again.'

'You could try and guess who I'm engaged to instead,' he retorted.

'I know already,' she said. 'You have to guess who I'm engaged to.'

'I don't have the energy at the moment,' he said. 'We'd better get our stuff together, I think, and go. You wouldn't mind ringing the station for me, would you? I need to know the train times. Do me that favour, please. I'm so tired.'

'I'll give you the answer, then,' she said. 'I'm engaged to you.'

He heard what she said. He heard it word by word but didn't grasp the meaning. He looked her in the eye, he looked at the table-cloth, he looked out of the window, he looked at the restaurant floor, and then he looked at the waiter who was hovering. He managed to give the waiter an order: two glasses, the same as before.

The waiter brought their drinks. They drank them in silence.

'Is it true?' Vatanen asked after a long interval.

Yes indeed, she affirmed. Vatanen had proposed in Kerava, and she had accepted in Turenki. The ring had been bought in Hanko. As the shops were closed, nothing better was obtainable. He'd bought it off a Hanko taxi-driver's daughter, a girl of eleven. Nickel, gold-plated nickel, Leila said.

'Really.'

'Yes.'

'So we're going to get married?' he asked.

'That's what you've been insisting, over and over, for days.'

So here he was, in yet another situation. The hare was not here, but in its place there was . . . this woman. Leila. Rather young, and lovely. His body thrilled with happiness, and a flush of power went through him: a woman, a woman had come to him! Young, healthy and vital! He wanted to take a closer look.

She was smart, desirable. Beautiful hands, long fingers. He held them, squeezed them tentatively. Nice, very nice. Her face was alluring – a perfect nose, and blue-grey eyes, rather large, no make-up, but long lashes . . . delightful, her mouth large, good, good, and such lovely teeth!

'Hm! You wouldn't mind getting me the papers?' he asked. He'd no need of papers: it was a stratagem to make her move. He wanted to watch her rise from the table, see her whole body walking across the room. He loved the way she rose from the chair: her hair bobbed adorably over the table as she turned.

To this extent, everything was ideal.

As she went to the newspaper-rack by the door, it was obvious how lovely her figure was, perhaps best of all. A massive joy flooded Vatanen's weary heart. And as she came back, he noticed how womanly her hips were: she swayed like a ship of dreams! Marvellous! Wonderful!

He didn't look at the papers. He thrust them aside and took her by the hand.

'I'm already married.'

'That makes you both married and engaged,' she said. It seemed to be all the same to her.

'You knew?'

'I know everything about you. I've been listening to you for over a week! You can't imagine how well I know you. And I'm counting on this: we'll be married some day, and you're going to come and live with me.'

'But supposing my wife won't give me a divorce?' he asked, knowing his own wife.

'She will. I'm a lawyer,' Leila said. 'But first of all there's another little matter: you'll have to give me complete power of attorney. You may not recall it, but in Helsinki you beat someone up: the secretary of the Junior League of the Coalition Party, and you made rather a mess of him. I'm going to take the case on. I doubt you'll be sentenced for a first offence.'

20 Humiliation

Vatanen took a dive into the slushy snow. A shot rang out, very close, then another. Buckshot fusilladed into the spruce trees. He dared not move. He could hear the irritable mumbling of drunken men.

'Blast it, he's done a blue streak.'

'Unless we dropped him.'

Their voices moved farther away, but Vatanen didn't dare get up or try to make off yet.

Things had taken a very nasty turn. The hare was fleeing through the Karjalohja forest with two great hounds at its heels, and Vatanen was crouched near a hummock in fear of his life.

How on earth had it got to this?

Vatanen and Leila had left Turku to spend the New Year in Helsinki. Her holiday over, Leila went back to work. Vatanen signed the power of attorney and moved in with her. After a week or two, he got a job repairing a summer villa at Karjalohja, a lakeside hamlet about fifty miles from Helsinki. A room required wallpapering, and the sauna was in a bad state inside and needed fixing up. A nice job for wintertime. He settled into the villa with the hare.

Now it was February already, and the previous evening a rowdy, disagreeable crowd had rolled up, out for a whale of a time in the villa next door. They heated the sauna and started an all-night rave-up. Men, and women with them, dashed naked on to the frozen lake, skidding and going for a drunken burton on the slippery ice; car engines revved all night long in the floodlit drive – off for more drink, or fetching up with more guests. The veranda was loud with endless yammer – the threat of communism in Finland and the free world, and so on – and now and then there were scuffles. Vatanen didn't get a wink all night, and the hare was on edge. Annoying headlights beamed across the walls and ceiling, and it was five o'clock before things settled down and the row petered out.

Around noon, things began to stir again. Crapulous voices moaned for a sauna: they had to get it going again or they'd never face the day.

The wood must have been used up the night before, and the drink finished as well, for two men called at Vatanen's door, asking the loan of some wood.

'We've come to get some sauna wood off you.'

'And a drop of the old stuff if you have some.'

Vatanen had neither sauna wood nor alcohol, and anyway he was in no mood to be friendly to the ravers of the night before. He pointed to the oil-stove and told them there was no wood: the sauna was being repaired.

'But listen, chum. We've got to have that wood. We're having a sauna, you see, we've made up our minds. Here's fifty quid. Now, what about that wood?'

Vatanen shook his head.

'Oh, a bit high and mighty, are we?' the other said. He threw some more notes on the table. 'Now! Let's have that wood, shall we? You could chop a bit off those veranda railings, for instance. You've got a saw. So what are you shaking your wig about? The money's there on the table.'

Vatanen had no intention of chopping up the house to please them, and they'd no intention of leaving it at that. Slamming some more notes on the table, they returned to the point: he'd better find some wood. Vatanen screwed up the notes, pushed them into the nearest man's breast-pocket and ordered them out.

'Christ, what next? What the bloody hell do you think you're doing?'

Vatanen was steering the men outside and closing the door. They started hammering on the door. When Vatanen didn't open it, one of them kicked the veranda rail and dislodged it. The other, eager to have a go, tore it completely loose, and it dropped into the yard. They grabbed hold of the wood and dragged it exultantly off to their own compound. Vatanen ran out to stop them, but they were already there.

'It's a co-operative!' one of the men yelled. 'We've created a co-operative!'

'Or, put it this way,' the other gloated. 'It's good business – if you can't buy it, take it.'

Standing at the edge of his compound, in a black rage, Vatanen watched the veranda-rail turning to firewood. A dozen other morning-after-the-night-befores came out to laugh and jeer. Someone set off in a car; someone else shouted: 'Get enough of the stuff this time! We don't want to run out!'

Rigid with rage, Vatanen stalked into the neighbour's compound and asked whom the house belonged to.

The chopping stopped. A fat, mulberry-faced man, who'd been busy splitting the railing, stretched up to his full height.

'Listen, chum, it belongs to some big fish. If you know what's good for you, you'll make tracks while you still can. I'm in charge here, and if you don't piss off I'll have the lads speeding your arse.'

'I'm going nowhere till this is settled,' Vatanen said, without any urgency.

The man bounced into the house and reappeared a moment later with a shotgun. He loaded both barrels on the steps and levelled the gun at Vatanen's chest. The nauseating stink of stale alcohol wafted on the air.

Suddenly one of the men who'd gathered round Vatanen kicked his backside so hard he was knocked flying on to his belly. An explosion of laughter broke out, and someone kicked him in the ribs.

He got to his feet. The women threw dirty sand-laden slush in his eyes; someone punched him in the back.

There was nothing for it but retreat to his own territory. Raucous laughter pursued him as he withdrew into the villa. Maybe, someone said, they'd gone a bit too far now; but the others disagreed.

'Shit! A bastard like that? He'll not chance his arm with the police. I tell you what we'll do. We'll put the frighteners on him. You'll not hear another squeak after that. But first, sauna! To work, men!'

Easy to imagine how sore Vatanen was: he took the hare in his arms and went out on to the ice, thinking he'd take a walk across the bay, sort his thoughts out and calm down. It was about half a mile to the farther shore.

When he was half-way across, the ravers loosed a couple of

large hounds at him. They'd spotted the hare he was carrying. 'After 'em! After 'em!' they shouted.

The yelping hounds tore across the ice in hot pursuit. The hare took to its heels, and, seeing it on the run, the hounds broke into a fierce baying. Their big paws slithered on the ice as they hurtled past Vatanen and vanished into the trees across the bay.

Vatanen pursued them to the headland, wondering how he could save his hare. What he needed was a gun, but that was hanging on a nail at Läähkimä Gulf.

Several men came running out of the villa, carrying guns. Bellowing as they ran, they were like the hounds they'd loosed. The ice bent under their weight.

Vatanen concealed himself among the trees, for as soon as they got to the headland, they fired in his direction. He was lying in the slushy snow, hearing the peevish mumbling of drunken men.

The hare was already far off, the baying of the hounds scarcely audible. Their cry was actually a howl; so the hunt was still on, the hare still alive.

Vatanen's brain was working overtime. This savage chase must stop, but how? How could such men exist? Where was the pleasure in a rough-house like this? How could human beings lower themselves so viciously?

The poor hare was circling back in its terror. Suddenly it burst out of a gap in the trees, saw Vatanen and dashed straight into his arms. Two drops of bright red blood had oozed from its mouth. The baying of the hounds was getting louder.

He knew the hounds could rip the life out of him if he stood there in the forest with a hunted hare in his arms. Should he reject his beloved beast? Send it on its way, save his own skin?

No – the thought shamed him as soon as it came. He ran for a knoll, overgrown with thick-boled, gnarled and twisted pines. Quickly he clambered on one. It was tricky, climbing with a hare in his arms: bits of fur got stuck on the bark; but he was out of reach when the hounds came whirling up, snorting and sniffing the hare's traces. They soon found their way to the foot of the tree and frenziedly reached up on their hind legs, yelping into the branches, clawing at the red bark with their paws. The hare thrust its head under Vatanen's armpit, trembling all over.

Boozy voices were again drawing nearer, and soon five men stood at the foot of the tree.

'Sit, boys, sit! So he's perched up there, is he, our friend – in the tree?'

They cackled, one kicked the tree-trunk, another tried rocking the tree to make Vatanen fall down.

'Losing his nerve, is he? Drop that bloody hare down here, or we'll have to pot it in your arms!'

'Let rip into the tree! Go on, have a go! Hell of a good story, that. Can you believe it? Karlsson shot a hare up a pine tree!'

'And got a Joe with the same shot!'

They were having a good old time. They pounded on the tree. The hounds slunk round the men's legs. Vatanen was so incensed, tears started to his eyes. Someone noticed.

'Shit, let's go, the bugger's crying. That's enough of a shindig for one Sunday, anyway.'

'But let him have the hounds for an hour: that'll teach him to beat his gums more politely next time. Come on. Sauna's waiting. It'll be hot already.'

They left. The hounds prowled on guard at the foot of the tree, barking and howling. Vatanen thought he was going to vomit.

Shortly before dark someone whistled the hounds away. They loped off reluctantly. Vatanen felt dizzy; the hare was still trembling.

He went back to Helsinki the same evening. At first he thought of bringing criminal charges, but in the end he didn't. To Leila he said: 'I'm off back north, to Läähkimä Gorge. It doesn't suit me down south.'

And off he went.

21 A Visit

Spring was here. Time flowed by pleasantly in the clean-aired northern climate. The chairman of the Reindeer Owners' Association had offered Vatanen a job constructing an enclosure for reindeer, and now he was hewing palings. The work was agreeably heavy, and free of constraint: he felt his own man. The hare was enjoying its existence at Läähkimä Gorge; the wild surroundings were scattered with its traces.

Leila kept him posted with letters: sometimes they arrived two at a time, for delivery was only every other week. Leila's letters were steamy, and it was distinctly enjoyable reading them. He replied less frequently, but enough to keep the fire going, so to speak. Leila hoped he'd give up Lapland and return at long last to the civilized world, but he couldn't make up his mind. He felt a diffidence about the south: the manners in conurbations disgusted him.

In the last week of March, life at Läähkimä Gorge altered dramatically.

Last autumn's bear had emerged from its lair – or perhaps it had not even tried to hibernate again after the pre-Christmas upsets. At any rate, the bear was once more on the prowl around Läähkimä Gorge. It had killed several reindeer, Vatanen observed: the soggy slush must have made it difficult for it to find other food. It came snuffling around the cabin walls, urinated at the corners and snorted testily in the March night.

These nocturnal visits rattled Vatanen, who slept in a bunk next to the log wall. The grunting and snorting on the other side of the wall made it difficult to sleep. He felt like a small fish in a fishtrap, with a big pike circling round.

Reason told him that bears don't attack human beings, but sometimes events are unreasonable.

For instance, one night the bear pushed a whole window in, frame and all. It thrust its upper body through the space, sniffing the warm air inside. Outside, there was a brilliant full moon, but the bear's body obstructed the whole window-space. The hare hopped on to Vatanen's bunk and cowered squeaking behind his back. Vatanen lay stiff. Quite a situation.

The bear snuffed the food left on the table – the remains of supper: dried reindeer meat, bread, butter, a bottle of tomato sauce, and a few other items. In the moonlight Vatanen saw the animal reach over from the window and adroitly paw some delicacies into its mouth. It rustled the wrappings and opened them out; then there were some smacking noises. How handy it was with its paws! Soon everything had been eaten, and the bear eased itself back for a moment into the yard.

When it appeared again, it was bolder. Its eye fell once more on the open tomato-sauce bottle: it picked it up in its paws and examined it, wondering. The smell seemed alluring. It kept squeezing the bottle, evidently not understanding how to extract the contents.

The bear gave it a shake. There was a splosh and a surprised groan as sauce flew out of the bottle and sprinkled the wall above Vatanen's head.

Now the bear appeared to be licking the bottle. In between, it squirted the sauce round the room, undoubtedly smearing itself all over in the process. It licked its coat. The sound reminded Vatanen of the name of the place, Läähkimä Gorge – 'Gasping Gorge': there was plenty of gasping going on at the moment.

Now the bear was licking the table-top. The oilcloth wrinkled under its thick tongue. The streaks of tomato sauce tempted it ever farther in: the window-opening was stuffed tight as a bottle with a bottle-brush. The bear's upper body was weighing on the table: the table collapsed, and the bear thumped on to the cabin floor in a clatter of shattering wood. It appeared somewhat shocked at first but soon recovered. It began exploring the interior of the cabin.

Vatanen was afraid to move a muscle.

The bear began licking the floor: the sauce had flown quite a distance. The moonlight illuminated the huge, lithe animal: a terrifying spectacle. Its massive head crossed the floor at licking-pace like an alarming cleaning-machine getting closer and closer to Vatanen's feet.

At this point the hare's nerves snapped. It hopped from Vatanen's back on to the floor and zigzagged round the room. The bear made a grab for it but was left groping, while the hare cowered inaccessibly in a recess.

The bear forgot it and began licking the wall at the foot of Vatanen's bed.

Only now did it notice the man. Cautiously and curiously, it began a puzzled examination. Hot, moist bear's breath warmed Vatanen's face. Feeling Vatanen's breath on its muzzle, the bear snorted, picked him up in his paws and shook him a little. Vatanen faked limpness, trying to appear unconscious.

The bear studied the body in its arms, somewhat like an ogre that had got hold of a doll and didn't know what to do with it. Tentatively it took a bite at Vatanen's stomach and brought about a stabbing cry of pain. Shocked, the bear threw the man against the cabin wall and fled through the window, out into the open air.

Vatanen felt his stomach. He was seeing pink and white stars, and his stomach was wet. Had it disembowelled him? Horror! He reached for his gun, crouched out into the yard and fired into the darkness. The bear had fled. The moon was shining.

He went back in, lit a lantern and examined his stomach. It was slippery with blood and bear-slobber, but nothing lethal, it seemed. The bear had bitten experimentally: actually, it was more of a nip. He was not disembowelled.

The hare was limping. The bear must have stepped on it accidentally, for if it had struck a blow, the hare would undoubtedly have been smashed to a pulp against the wall.

Vatanen kicked the remains of the table against the wall, nailed a blanket across the window, and bandaged a sheet round his stomach. The wound ached: the bear had lacerated him enough for that.

He picked the hare up and hugged it. He stroked its innocent white coat and promised: 'Before dawn tomorrow, I'll be off on that bear's tracks. It's had it.'

The hare's sensitive white whiskers trembled earnestly: it looked as though it agreed: the bear had to be killed! A hare was thirsting after a bear's blood!

22 The White Sea

The moon set. Vatanen stuffed his knapsack with several days' provisions, thrust twenty cartridges into the flap-pocket, loaded his gun and sharpened his axe. He packed five packets of cigarettes for good measure, some matches and some ski-wax. To the hare he said: 'You'll be coming along too, won't you?' He left a note on the table, saying: *I'm off after a bear. May be gone a few days.*
– Vatanen

He closed the bunkhouse door behind him, waxed his skis, fitted them on and shouldered his knapsack and his gun. There were bear-tracks all over the place, but in spite of the dark he identified fresh tracks farther out, showing the bear leaving at a high trot. He pushed off on their trail; the snow was pretty firm under his skis.

'Now, Mr Bloody Bear, we'll see.'

The tracks led across the gorge itself. Vatanen ski'd off at a strong and even pace; his back began to sweat under the pressure of the knapsack. The hare limped along at his side.

The March sun rose into a brilliant sky. The air was exhilaratingly crisp; the snow squeaked as the sticks prodded; skiing conditions were excellent. He relished the going and the glittering snow – so bright in the rising sun, it made his forehead ache if he opened his eyes wide.

The tracks showed the bear had calmed down: probably it felt it had got away. Vatanen speeded up: he might well catch up with his quarry.

In the afternoon he swooped into a thick grove of spruce and saw that the bear had been lying down there. It may have heard the skis coming and taken to its heels. More skiing, that meant, perhaps many days of it before he caught up with the beast, if then. Fortunately, the snow gave way under the bear more than under the skier.

He came to an open sweep of marshland, where the tracks led south. Across a prospect of six or seven miles he glimpsed his quarry: the bear was a little black dot slinking into snowy forest at the far side. That spurred him on. Thrusting hard, he flew across the flats.

The sun went down. Where the underlying growth was thickest, the tracks were hard to make out. It was time to stop and eat. He felled a large dead tree and made a fire from the top branches; he fried some reindeer meat in his pan, drank some tea and slept for a few hours. When he woke, the moon had risen in a perfectly clear sky; it was possible to follow the tracks again.

The brilliant night and snowy Lapland wilderness had a cruel beauty. It was too exciting to feel fatigue. Sweat froze on his back as the frost took hold. His lashes froze, clogging his eyes: he had to take off a glove from time to time and melt the clots with his hand. Occasionally the hare started nibbling edible bits from brookside osier bushes. 'Careful! Don't get left behind,' Vatanen warned. 'This is no time to eat.'

Twice the bear had lain down: it must be tiring. But each time it had evidently heard the skis through the crisp night air and had made off. Now it was heading south-east. In a single day they'd crossed the Tanhua road; now they were approaching the great north-eastern wilderness, with its fells. They'd been over many rivers that night; at one point the snow had melted and the bear had drunk the ice-cold water. Vatanen bypassed the spot carefully: it would have been death to ski inadvertently into the icy black water.

The moon set; it was dark; he had to stop. He made a fire and slept in its warmth. The hare nibbled a little and then dropped off to sleep too.

When the sun rose, Vatanen set off again. They were somewhere in the desolate wilderness west of the tiny hamlet of Martti. Now, he worked out, they must be heading towards the parish of Savukoski. The bear seemed to be running straight to the little village itself. Soon they should hit the highway; and soon, there it was, the road. The bear had crossed the Savukoski–Martti road about half-way between the two villages. The ridges thrown up by the snow-ploughs had exasperated the beast: it had torn up the road sign as it went by and bent it over like a twig: a sort of message to Vatanen: 'Human, I've got all my power still. Keep off!'

But Vatanen continued his pursuit.

In the afternoon the sun turned the snow slushy. It began to stick to the skis, and the going became all puffing and blowing. The tracks in the snow were fresh, but progress was beginning to seem hopeless. Snow caked the skis to the point where he had to break off.

The snow didn't harden till evening. Then Vatanen ski'd a couple of hours, but it became too dark to see: this night there was no moon. He had to spend the night by his camp-fire. He guessed he was already in the parish of Salla, at most twenty-odd miles from the Soviet frontier. The hare was tired out, but it didn't complain: it never did moan about its lot. Vatanen felled an aspen sapling and split the bark with his axe. The hare ate and then collapsed into sleep, legs stretched, warming its belly in the fire's circle of light. Never before had the hare seemed so tired.

'I wonder if the pace is as punishing for the bear?'

As soon as there was light enough to see the tracks again, Vatanen continued his pursuit. The knapsack was lightweight, the food finished. Now he was in a hurry: the bear had to be killed before it reached the Soviet frontier. The trail was leading through the northern regions of the Tenniönjoki river valley towards the hamlet of Naruska, he estimated. He'd ski'd off the limits of his maps a few days earlier: now he had to rely on his memory of the overall map of Finland. The village of Salla itself, he knew, was a mere twelve miles from the border.

It was a dragging, gruelling day.

In the evening he was just south of Karhuntunturi – 'Bear Fell'! He gave up the trail and took the road to a village. He was so tired he had a fall on the slippery, snow-ploughed road. Children came out of the hamlet to meet him, and they all greeted him, for it's the custom in the north for children to greet adults. He asked where the shop was.

But the shop had closed down long ago. A mobile shop drove up twice a week. Vatanen took his skis off and called at the house next to the old shop. The man of the house was having a meal in the living-room; his wife was peeling hot potatoes near the stove and taking them to her husband one at a time.

An exhausted man looks, in a way, alarming, and yet not an

immediate threat. He has rights in the north, which people observe
with an intuitive discretion. The host gestured to the chair beside
him and invited Vatanen to eat.

Vatanen did eat. He was so tired the spoon shook to the beat of
his heart. He'd forgotten to take his cap off. The reindeer stew
was delicious and substantial. He ate the lot.

'So when does the mobile shop come?' he asked.

'Be here tomorrow.'

'I'm in a rush. You couldn't let me have a few days' food yourself, could you?'

'Where've you ski'd from?'

'From Sompio. Läähkimä Gorge.'

'Is it a wolverine you're after?'

'Something of the sort.'

The children came in and started a hullabaloo. The host ordered
them out and took Vatanen to a bedroom. He drew back the coun-
terpane from a double bed and told Vatanen to get some sleep.
Vatanen could hear him instructing his wife in the living-room:
'Put four days' food in a bag and tell the children to be quiet out
there. I'll wake him after a bit.'

A couple of hours later Vatanen came to without anyone waking him. He realized he'd been sleeping on top of the sheets, fully
clothed, with his boots on. In the living-room the children were
stroking the hare. When they saw Vatanen was awake, they began
chattering.

Vatanen put some money on the table, but the host handed it
back. They went outside. He felt stiff; his stomach was hurting.

'You haven't got any boracic acid, have you?'

'Leena, go and get some antiseptic off your mother'.

The girl ran in and came out again with a bottle. Vatanen opened
his trousers and his host saw the tooth-marks.

'A hellish big mouth it had!'

The host dressed the inflamed bite with the antiseptic and circled Vatanen's stomach two or three times with gauze. Then Vatanen
set off to pick up the trail again. From the edge of the forest he
called back: 'Is this Kotala or Naruska?'

'This is Naruska!'

Soon he found the trail, and the contest was on again.

He could see that the bear was tired and in a fury: it had been
slashing trees that were in its way with its claws; it had bashed

down several dead trees; chips of wood had been flying around everywhere. Was the bear, Vatanen wondered, going to disappear over the frontier?

'But nothing'll save you now, mister. No good defecting to a great power.'

In the night a freezing wind blew up. The clouds allowed only occasional glimpses of the moon. He was forced to stop for the hours of night. In the morning the wind had swept the tracks clean: he had to ski hither and thither before he located some fresh tracks among the snow.

How many days was it now? It no longer mattered.

He pushed the worn-out hare into his knapsack and set off again. Snow was falling more and more, and it became a storm. In the whirl it was difficult to see the tracks, even though they were fresh. If he stopped the pursuit now, he knew, the whole trip would be a flop. His stomach was hurting him; the gauze had slipped down to his groin, but he couldn't afford the time to adjust it.

The tracks climbed a fell-side. Here the wind was fit to buffet the sweating man over, but he soldiered on. He had to! Now his eyes, he noticed, seemed to be failing him. Was he getting snow-blind after all the days and days of staring at tracks? More than likely.

'But you'll not escape my claws, you devil!'

It was dreadful weather: the storm stopped him seeing more than a yard or two ahead. Mechanically, he traced the powdering-over tracks. Gone was that joy he'd felt at the start. All day long the storm raged. He was no longer sure which way he was going, but he fastened on to the tracks like a leech. As he went, he occasionally sucked on some Naruska pork fat, now frozen solid, or clawed some of the snow stuck to his shoulders to quench his thirst. Then, suddenly, the tracks dropped out of the forest on to the snow-ploughed road. The bear had got so tired, it had taken to running along the highway.

It had been skidding on the icy surface: there were great claw-marks in the blowing snow. Vatanen shuddered. An icy chill went down his spine.

He came to a crossroads, with signposts. Excellent! Now he could find out where he was.

He stopped and, leaning heavily on his ski-sticks, began peering at the signs. But he didn't understand the language.

He'd ski'd across the border into Soviet Russia. The signposts were Russian, the script Cyrillic. The surprise made sweat break out on his brow.

Should he turn back now? Should he report to the Soviet authorities?

'So this is where we are, dammit!'

His indecision at the crossroads was short. He pushed off again in pursuit, skiing doggedly till evening, when he did get a glimpse of his quarry; but then darkness covered the beast. Again he felled a pine, made a camp-fire and settled down for the night, his first in Soviet territory. Ahead of him were the immeasurable forest wildernesses of the Kola peninsula and the White Sea: they'd test his blood.

The next day the weather improved a little, and Vatanen charged along like a mad bull. He crossed several large roads, with the bear tending eastwards and showing no sign of ever turning westwards. From the south, a supersonic aircraft sped overhead, off to Murmansk. He had to stop and look at the glittering-winged, faster-than-sound projectile. It made a deep impact on an exhausted skier: what different modes of transport human beings had!

The bear was avoiding villages and making its way through the deserted places. Vatanen didn't encounter a single soul but did cross several ski-tracks in the wilderness. Could his violation of the frontier have passed unobserved? Possibly: in the storm Vatanen himself hadn't noticed the boundary. Talk of an iron curtain was evidently misplaced: there'd not been a single strand of barbed wire to snag his skis.

His food had run out two days earlier, but the hunt went on. He came to a hamlet. The bear had slept the night in the ruin of a stone building, evidently an old salt boilery, Vatanen concluded. That meant they were getting close to the sea: the White Sea.

He burst upon the Murmansk railway-line. His skis clanked in the frosty air as he made his way over the many pairs of rails. The track was electrified – which called for caution as he hurried by.

His only nourishment was some pork rind he'd boiled the previous evening. He was hungry, but nothing but the bear mattered to him now.

And then, there was the sea-shore: the bear was dashing on to the ice; far out a black ice-breaker had several small cargo ships trailing in its channel.

The bear was scudding across the ice of the Gulf of Kandalaksk, with Vatanen in hot pursuit. A few miles north, the factory chimneys of Kandalaksha were staining the clear, frosty sky. The bear, with Vatanen after it, loped up to the ice-breaker's channel: the last battle of this fearful trek was being waged on the dazzlingly immaculate ice of the White Sea.

The bear rose on its hind legs at the edge of the channel. It gave a howl and a roar: the brilliant white neckband in its black coat flashed in the sun. The bear turned on its pursuer, bellowing outrage and hatred. Vatanen took off his skis; he lay prone on the ice, melted the rime on the rifle with his thumb, released the safety-catch and shot the bear right in the chest.

The great bear collapsed on the ice: no second shot was needed. Vatanen crawled up to the bear, opened its gullet and let the blood flow out, black and clotted. He cupped his hands and supped two handfuls. Then he sat on the huge carcass and lit a cigarette, his last. He wept; he didn't know why, but the tears came. He stroked the bear's fur, stroked his hare, which was lying in his knapsack with its eyes closed.

Two large aeroplanes landed on the ice, and soldiers leaped out. About twenty men came over to Vatanen, and one of them addressed him in the Russianized Soviet-Karelian Finnish dialect: 'So well, comrade, you got it! On behalf Red Army, congratulations! Now I arrest you as spy. But no worry – this formality. Have drink.'

A burning-cold swig of vodka took the tears from Vatanen's eyes. He introduced himself and said: 'Excuse me for crossing the border, but otherwise I wouldn't have got this bear.'

'Vot! comrade, excused! Some ski-trip! Now, into plane. These men skin bear. You bringing this hare with you?'

They embarked, and the aircraft left the ice. A few minutes later it landed on a mainland airstrip.

'Vot! first sauna, then sleep. Interrogation tomorrow.'

23 In Government Hands

Vatanen and the hare were held in custody in the Soviet-Karelian ASSR for two months. During this period Vatanen was interrogated several times and probed for information about Finland. It emerged that the Soviet frontier troops had tracked his crossing of the frontier and kept his ski journey under continuous observation day by day as far as the White Sea.

Vatanen had been mentioned on Karelian ASSR radio. The *Karelian ASSR News* interviewed him, and photographs showed him bearskin on shoulder, with the hare under his arm.

All the officials were well disposed. He was not confined to prison but permitted to walk about freely in the streets of Petrozavodsk, after giving his word that he would not attempt to ski to Finland before the formalities were completed.

Finland was sent a two-hundred-page interrogation report. It included a detailed account of Vatanen's movements on both sides of the border. The Soviet authorities in Petrozavodsk requested the Finnish Minister of the Interior to investigate the validity of Vatanen's statements. A month later Petrozavodsk received a reply from the Finnish authorities confirming the correctness of Vatanen's statements; the document pointed out that Vatanen had been charged with a large number of crimes in Finland.

Vatanen had (1) committed adultery. He had misled the authorities by (2) not providing notice of removal on (3) deserting his family the previous summer. He was consequently (4) a vagrant. (5) He had retained a protected wild animal in his possession for several days without a valid permit. (6) In Nilsiä, Vatanen, together with a certain Hannikainen, had engaged in clandestine jacklightfishing and other piscatorial ventures without a permit. (7) In the course of a forest fire he had contravened the alcohol regulations by knowingly consuming an illegally distilled spirituous liquor. (8) Additionally during the said forest fire, he had neglected his duties over a twenty-four-hour period while consuming alcohol with a certain Salosensaari. (9) In Kuhmo he had desecrated a recently deceased body. (10) At the village of Meltaus on the River Ounasjoki, he had been party to unlawful appropriation and illegal sale of German war booty. (11) In Posio, he had been guilty of cruelty to animals. (12) At Vittumainen Ghyll he had inflicted grievous bodily harm on a skiing instructor named Kaartinen. (13) He was charged with neglecting to give due and timely warning of a dangerous bear inhabiting the vicinity of Läähkimä Gorge, Sompio. (14) At Sompio, he had also contravened the law by taking part in a bear-hunt without a permit to carry a weapon. (15) At Vittumainen Ghyll, he had obtruded without invitation on a state occasion organized by the Minister for Foreign Affairs. (16) Under false pretences, he had obtained treatment for the hare in his possession at the National Institute of Veterinary Science, Helsinki, a state research institute, and, furthermore, had failed to provide monetary compensation. (17) He had assaulted the Secretary of the Coalition Party's Junior League in the WC of a Helsinki restaurant and inflicted grievous bodily harm. (18) He had endangered life by riding a bicycle in an inebriated condition on the major road to Kerava. (19) While travelling between Turenki and Hanko, he had illegally become engaged to a certain Heikkinen while already married. (20) In Sompio, he had for a second time committed the offence of bear-hunting without a permit to carry a weapon. (21) In the course of hunting a protected animal he had violated the frontier of the Soviet Union without a passport or relevant visa. Thereafter (22), he had been guilty of the crimes which he had confessed to the Soviet authorities.

The document indicated that because of the diverse criminal charges against him, Vatanen would be brought before the Finnish courts for trial and sentence. His extradition was requested. It was also requested that the pelt of the bear he had killed be returned to Finland, and that the wild hare in Vatanen's possession be returned to Finland.

'Quite a record!' chuckled the interrogator in Petrozavodsk. 'All I can do now is hand you over to the government in Leningrad.

Let them sort you out.'

In Leningrad Vatanen was given a room in the Astoria Hotel while the Soviet Union was clarifying the situation from their point of view. The Soviet authorities relinquished any further claims on Vatanen and, at last, on 13 June, he was escorted to the station to be put on the train for Finland. The major who accompanied him to the station hugged him fiercely, kissed him on both cheeks, and said: 'Comrade, when you getting free, vot! You come back Astoria. We drink together!'

24 Afterword

This is how it went with Vatanen: once over the border, he was arrested at the frontier town of Vainikkala, locked in a cellpod in an armoured prisoner-conveyance van, and transported to Helsinki. The hare was also delivered there in a plywood box with round holes in the sides and the word *Animal* on the lid.

In remand, Vatanen gave some thought to his situation but showed no remorse. On the contrary he hardened under detention, so that even the mild-eyed prison chaplain shook his head, swallowing hard.

The hare constituted a problem for the authorities: it was undoubtedly Vatanen's property and could not be slaughtered or eaten. Through his lawyer, Vatanen appealed for the hare to face charges as an accomplice in all the crimes, hoping thus to get the beloved creature to share his cell and comfort him during his imprisonment.

The director of Prison Administration studied the legalities and came to his conclusion: if Vatanen were a woman and the hare his baby, the baby could indeed share the cell with the mother till it was weaned and viable without her; but in Finland an animal did not come into this category. A wild hare could not, in any strict meaning of the term, be regarded as Vatanen's pet; but the director of Prison Administration had to point out that, in any case, the companionship of pets, or comparable animals, was forbidden to prisoners. In addition, the prevention of Cruelty to Animals Act made the incarceration of a hare with Vatanen unlawful, as a prison cell was rated an unwholesome environment for a wild animal, which, juridically, Vatanen's hare could still be considered to be. This being the case, the director of Prison Administration disallowed admission of the hare to the cell, and indeed the animal would be at risk of perishing there.

'You see, this cell of yours is too gloomy for an innocent animal,' the chaplain explained when he brought Vatanen the official decision.

The matter was put right only when Vatanen wrote a letter to the President of the Republic. To smuggle the letter outside the prison walls, he stuck it to the bottom of a food-bowl on its way to the galvanizing plant, where one of the staff swallowed the letter and, after evacuating it in his flatlet the same evening, dried the document, smoothed it, put it into a clean envelope, and slipped it in the presidential palace post-box in the middle of a moonlight night. It was removed at precisely six o'clock the following morning and placed on the presidential desk in the secretariat.

Hardly an hour and ten minutes after the unsealing of the envelope, the hare was delivered to Vatanen's cell in a chip basket.

When I, the author of the present book, tried to quiz Vatanen about how he had managed to effect this, he said he didn't want to go into further detail: the letter had been intended as confidential from the start.

For myself, it was an exceptional privilege to contact Vatanen during the custodial police enquiries. We had extensive exchanges, on which I made the most detailed possible minutes, and it is on the basis of these that I have written the present book.

The image that has impressed itself on my mind is of a man, in many respects, profound in reflection, benevolent in disposition. Never shall I forget his final words at the conclusion of our last interview: 'Such is life.'

As I see it, Vatanen's personal history and manner of conduct reveal him to be a revolutionary, a true subversive, and therein lies the secret of his greatness. Watching Vatanen tenderly stroking the hare's fur in his dismal cell, as if he were its dam, I was aware of what human solidarity may entail. I remember certain moments when, as the moist-eyed prisoner looked at his stone wall, a vague intuition disturbed me: that nothing on earth could prevent this afflicted man from once more demonstrating the full force of his whole being.

The present volume was already going to press when an express telegram, expedited by mounted courier, arrived on my desk from the prison: Vatanen and the hare had escaped from gaol!

I rushed to the prison and ascertained how the break-out had occurred. It is one of the more remarkable events in our criminal history. Vatanen's longing for freedom was such that, one agonizing day, with the hare in his arms, he stepped through his cell-wall into the exercise yard, crossed the open space to the exterior wall, and walked through that too into the freedom beyond; and neither he nor the hare have been seen since. During these moments of flight, the prison warders were as if paralysed behind their machine-guns and harpoons – incapable of impeding his flight in any way.

Moreover, Vatanen's lawyer, L. Heikkinen, was not available the day after the escape, and there is still no information as to her whereabouts.

The last news alone shows that one cannot lightly engage with Vatanen.